W9-AEM-056

The Far Forests

ALSO BY JOAN AIKEN

Castle Barebane

Midnight Is a Place

The Mooncusser's Daughter
A PLAY FOR CHILDREN

The Skin Spinners
POEMS

JOAN AIKEN

The Far Forests

Tales of Romance,
Fantasy, and Suspense

THE VIKING PRESS NEW YORK

First Edition

First published in 1977 by The Viking Press
625 Madison Avenue, New York, N.Y. 10022
Printed in U.S.A.

1 2 3 4 5 81 80 79 78 77

Library of Congress Cataloging in Publication Data

Aiken, Joan, 1924– The far forests.

Summary: A collection of fifteen short stories of mystery, magic, and romance.
[1. Short stories] I. Title.
PZ7.A2695Far [Fic] 77–356
ISBN 0–670–30760–2

Contents

Lodging for the Night

"THIS sewing machine will last you over sixty years without needing repair or maintenance," said Henry Dulge. He took a quick look at the housewife; that should see her well into her hundred and twenties, he thought. "It is rustless, foolproof, perfectly insulated, five pounds down, and a hundred-and-forty-eight payments of ninety-nine and a half. I'll leave it with you for a week's trial, shall I? Or will you sign right away? Here's the form. . . ."

"It's ever so kind of you," she said faintly. "But in your advert that I saw it said—what I wrote up for was—"

"And of course that entitles you to free service and repair for the first two months, not that you are going to need that with an O-Sew-matic, ha ha!"

"You did say in your advert that you had reconditioned models for sale for eight pounds," she persisted timidly.

His face changed. "Oh, well, of course, if you want *that* sort of stuff— We did have just a few, but they're trash, let me assure you, madam, trash! Why, you'd only use one for a few days before you'd be begging me to change it for an O-Sew-matic. Now, this lovely model here, you can make all your children's clothes on it, curtains, quilts, it's like a dream to handle—"

"Haven't you one of the 8-pound models in your van that I could just look at?" she pleaded.

He hesitated. But it was pouring rain, and she looked the

sort that could be browbeaten—a pale, pulpy little woman with hair like tangled raffia. "No I haven't, as a matter of fact," he snapped. "Sold the last one to a silly old fool who didn't know a bad bargain when she saw one. Now you be sensible, madam, you take my advice, you'll never regret it—"

She wavered. "Well—I do want to get on with my husband's winter shirts—"

He handed her the pen.

At this critical moment her husband came home, beer-flavoured and hungry for his supper.

"What the blazes is going on here?" he growled, taking in the whole situation—the poised pen, the form with its mass of small print, the seductive glitter of the O-Sew-matic, and Henry Dulge's truculence suddenly turned ingratiating.

"I was just explaining to your good lady here—"

She gave her husband an alarmed, pleading smile, but he was wasting no time.

"Out! And take your flaming machine with you. I'll have no never-never in my house. *Out!*"

The rain blattered against the front window. Henry Dulge was not a coward. He rallied for a last try—but the husband moved towards him so threateningly that he abandoned the hope, picked up the O-Sew-matic, said, with an angry, pitying laugh, "Well, I'm afraid you're going to be very, very sorry for this, madam. You won't often get the chance of such a bargain," and departed, letting the wind slam the door behind him.

Rain sluiced over the aluminium cover of the O-Sew-matic, and he had to rub it dry, cursing, before he drove off into the drenching dusk. He was so annoyed at having missed what promised to be an easy sale that instead of finding a hotel for the night, as he had intended, he drove straight through the town and on along the coast road towards Crowbridge.

The rain spun down in his headlights, thick as thatch, and bounced off the shingle-spattered road. Every half mile or so illuminated signs by the roadside warned: THIS ROAD IMPASSABLE DURING SPRING TIDES WHEN TIDE IS HIGH.

Dulge had no notion whether the tide was at spring or neap, but in any case it was satisfactorily far out—only occasionally when the road curved up over a bluff did he catch a glimpse of tossing, menacing whitecaps, far to his right.

He passed a solitary, plodding walker, a tramp, to judge from his pack and ragged coat, and took a mean pleasure in cutting close past the man to spray him with mud and sand from the wheels. The fellow must be soaked through, anyway; a bit extra wouldn't make much odds.

Ten miles farther on he overtook another pedestrian, this time a girl. She was wearing a dark rain cape but the headlights picked out the white kerchief over her hair. Henry's chivalry came to the fore, and he pulled in beside her and opened the door.

"Hop in, mermaid," he said jovially. She seemed startled, but thanked him, and settled quietly beside him. He let out the clutch, pleased with such a piece of luck: this girl was a peach, a real contest winner, looked a bit chilled with the wet and cold—what the devil was she doing walking along the coast road at this time of night?—but a topnotch figure, what he could see of it, and classy too, with that pale-gold hair trained back from a high forehead.

"Dangerous along here, didn't you know?" he said. "Wouldn't want the tide to come in and wash away a pretty girl like you."

"Oh, I often walk this way," she said carelessly. "There is no danger if you know the state of the tide."

"Live in Crowbridge?"

"Yes, I have a house there."

"All on your own?"

She nodded. His eyes widened. This seemed an unbelievably promising situation.

"That makes two of us then. Here's me, a poor bachelor, don't know a soul in the town. How about cheering me up? Have dinner with me at the Ship?"

"You are kind," she said, "but I never eat at inns."

"How about inviting me round to your place then? Take pity on the stranger, eh?"

She looked at him oddly. "I never invite guests. Those who wish for my hospitality must find the way themselves."

They had entered the small port of Crowbridge and were climbing the main street towards the upper town. Street lamps, wildly swinging from their brackets, threw shifting gleams of light on Tudor gables and brickwork.

"I won't be shy in finding the way, darling, believe me. What's you name? Where's your house?"

"I live near here," she said, "if you will be so kind as to put me down."

"Ah, come on now, darling. At least have a quick one with me at the old Ship, to keep out the wet."

"Thank you no, I—"

But he drove on. He was forced to stop, though, at the traffic lights, and to his annoyance she somehow managed to slip out—heaven knew how she did it, for he thought he had locked the door and that catch was the devil to shift anyway. Before he could let out a word or curse she was gone, following the flutter of her kerchief into the dark rainy night. The lights changed to green, and a furious hooting from behind forced him on, damning her wholeheartedly, the artful bitch! But Crowbridge was a small town; maybe someone at the pub would know who she was.

He made straight for the bar and had three doubles in quick succession to sink the memory of the missed sale and the mislaid pickup. Then he inquired about a bed for the night.

"Sorry, sir. I'm afraid we're full right up."

"Full up? In October? Are you crazy?"

"It's the annual conference of the NAFFU, sir. Always held in Crowbridge. I'm afraid you won't find a bed in the town. I know for a fact they're full at the Crown and the George, we've had people come on from there."

"For Pete's sake! Isn't there anywhere in the town I can get a bed—digs, boardinghouse, anything?" He appealed to the other drinkers in the bar. "Can't any of you gentlemen suggest somewhere? It's thirty miles on to Castlegate."

They hesitated. "The road's flooded too between here and Castlegate," put in the barman. "I doubt you'd not get through that way."

"Well," said one man after a pause, "he could sleep at the old Dormer House."

"What's that?" Henry's hopes rose. "A hostel?"

"No, it's a private house. As a matter of fact it's empty now—

due for demolition. Work starts tomorrow. The Council's been itching to get it out of the way for years, but they couldn't touch it till the last of the family died, which she did a couple of months back—an old lady of ninety-three. Historic sort of place. Some society's been protesting about the demolition, but the house sticks right out into a crossroads. Makes a very dangerous corner."

"Ah, well, some of these old places have to come down; can't keep 'em all," Henry agreed. "But I can't stay there if it's empty, can I? I don't fancy sleeping on bare boards."

"Ah, you see, that's the point It's a kind of a celebrated house, the old Dormer—you're sure you haven't heard of it?"

"No, never."

"There's a tradition that if anyone asks to stay, the family will allow them to—Hardisty, the family name was, belonged to the Hardistys since the first Queen Elizabeth's time—and give them free fire and bedding. A clause in the old lady's will, the Miss Hardisty who just died, said this custom was to be kept up till demolition began. So you'll find fires and beds there."

"Free fire and bedding? Sounds too good to be true! Maybe my luck's changing. And about time too."

"There's another thing."

"Well?"

"Anyone who stays there till eight o'clock next morning has a right to claim a thousand pounds from the estate."

"A *thousand pounds*? What do you think I am? A sucker?"

But all the men in the bar assured him that this was perfectly true. They were quite serious. Henry, studying the faces, began to believe them.

"But has nobody claimed it yet?"

"Not one. It's haunted, you see."

"Haunted? What by?" Henry looked sceptical. "I'd like to see the ghost that could shift *me* out of a free bed and a thousand quid."

"By one of the family, a girl called Bess Hardisty, who lived in the first Elizabeth's time. The story goes that her young man fell in love with the Queen. He was so dazzled that he went off and forgot Bess, sailed to discover the Indies and never came back. She turned bitter and sour, lived to be very old, and was finally burned as a witch. Since then no one but members of the family can sleep in the house—she gives people terrible dreams."

Henry burst out laughing. "She'll be clever if she can give me dreams! Why, it's a cinch. Can you do me dinner here?" he asked the barman.

"Why, yes, sir, we can manage that."

"All right, you give me some dinner, and then tell me where to find this place. By the way," he added, remembering, "can you tell me the name of a girl who lives on her own here, very pretty girl, about twenty-five, pale blond hair?"

"No, sir, I can't say I can call her to mind," said the barman. "But I haven't been here long." The other men shook their heads. Did some of them look at Henry oddly? It was probably his hunger that made him imagine them suddenly pale and remote, as if seen through glass; he would pursue the matter of the girl when he'd had a good dinner.

The Ship dinner was excellent, but the service was slow. It was near closing time when Henry returned to the bar, and by now he was feeling tired. The men who had been there before were gone now, and the barman seemed preoccupied. Why bother about the girl? If she was lost, she was lost, no sense whining over her. He had a couple more drinks fairly fast, put his car in the town car park, and took the direction the barman had given him.

The rain had let up a little, but it was still too dark to see much of the old Dormer House, and he was in no mood to linger. He pushed open the heavy door and climbed the stairs. No electricity, but he had his powerful car torch, and from somewhere above he could see the glow and hear the comfortable crackle of a blazing fire.

A few rooms he looked into were empty, already stripped of their furniture, but, following the firelight, he found a big stately bedroom with a carpet and chairs and a blue-silk-hung fourposter. It smelt delicious, of applewood and lavender. Henry dumped his wet case on the carpet with a grunt of content and punched the mattress.

"This certainly beats the old Ship," he said to himself with satisfaction. "I bet Queen Elizabeth never slept on *that*."

Apart from himself, the house seemed empty. He undressed

leisurely by the leaping fire, replenished it from a basket of logs, bolted the door, and got into bed. The bed was even warm—you might have thought one of those Elizabethan things—what did they call them?—warming pans, had just been taken out of it.

And when he was more than halfway into the mist of sleep, a pair of warm arms came round his neck and a voice said gently in his ear, "Did you think you weren't going to see me again? I knew you'd find your way here."

"Is that you, darling?" Henry murmured sleepily. "My luck surely has turned. But how did you get in? I could have sworn there was no one in the place."

"I was here already. Don't you see? I live here. . . ."

It was after him. It was gaining on him. A hundred, five hundred people, women mostly, were watching him with hating eyes, cheering it on, and it was plunging along the road behind him, its great wheel letting off blue sparks as it whirled round, the gigantic needle munching steadily towards him, cutting the tar of the road as if it were cheese. Now it was right alongside him and he was paralysed, unable to stir, and the needle was above him, vibrating, poised for the terrible downward thrust that would pierce from brain to groin, pinning him to the bed like a butterfly—

He woke sweating, screaming, struggling with the bedclothes. Instinctively he turned to seek the comfort of his bedmate, but she was gone. Could he feel something metallic, hard and ice cold among the sheets? He leapt out as if he had found a snake in the bed. The grip of nightmare was still on him and he started pulling on his clothes with frantic, trembling haste, all other considerations lost in the urge to get out of there. He kept glancing haggardly at the ceiling, as if he expected the great bright needle to come plunging through to impale him. The fire burned bright, but he never noticed the portrait on the wall of a pale, gilt-haired girl smiling primly above her ruff; he overlooked the scatter of clothes on a chair, the brocade skirts, the little square-toed shoes with jewelled buckles. He unbolted the door with shaking hands, stumbled down the stairs, and ran for the car park like a hunted thing. The rain had stopped, but dead leaves like packs of wolves scurried down the street after him and the wind shook and grappled him. Not a soul stirred; it was the dead hour of night.

He found a board across the Castlegate road: FLOODS. IMPASSABLE, and turned back the way he had come, along the coast road to Trowchester. The tide was nearly full now; he could hear the roar of the waves like a thousand sewing machines, and he cast a nervous glance in the rear mirror, half wondering if he would see *It* coming steadily along behind, munching up the miles. What a hell of a dream. He would have to pack in the job if he had many more like that.

When he turned his eyes back to the road ahead, he found the girl sitting in the car beside him.

He gasped something incoherent. His hands shook and slipped on the wheel.

"You didn't think I'd stay behind, did you?" she said. "I'm coming with you. They're pulling my house down tomorrow, I shall have nowhere to live. It was lucky you came to see me tonight. Now I can come and live in *your* house."

"You can't—you can't!" he gabbled. "I've a wife—children—"

He jabbed his foot on the accelerator, and the car swooped up over a bluff, following the old, winding coast road. But on the far side of the bluff there was no road, only the white-capped waves, warring with the dark of the night, grinding like a thousand sewing machines against the shingle bank. His car ran smoothly in among the crests and disappeared.

At about the same time two policemen were interrogating a tramp in the streets of Crowbridge.

"Let's have a look at that pack of yours," one of them said, mistrusting the raggedness of the man and the suspicious weight of the pack.

"I object," the tramp said with dignity. "It's starting to rain again and I don't want my things all wet."

"You'll have to come along to the station then."

He accompanied them without protest. He was a blue-eyed, weatherbeaten man who might have been any age between forty and seventy. His pack, opened at the police station, proved to contain sheets of paper covered with handwriting, and a number of books.

"Russian," whispered one of the constables. "Think he's a spy, sarge?"

"That's Greek, you ignorant thick," said the sergeant, who had been on Crete. "All right, you can go. Be a bit more co-operative another time."

"It's coming down hard now," the tramp said mildly. "I suppose you can't put me up for the night in a cell?"

"Sorry, mate, cells all full up with trade-union members sleeping it off."

"He could go to the Old Dormer," the constable said.

"Where's that?" the tramp asked.

The sergeant said doubtfully, "Well, I suppose it won't do no harm."

They told him how to get there.

It was raining hard again. The tramp made haste to get indoors but then, instead of going upstairs, found the big stone-flagged kitchen with its massive table, and pulled up a chair. He took a piece of paper, a pencil, and a lump of cheese from his pack, and began writing slowly, with many crossings-out, absently taking a bite of cheese from time to time.

About half an hour later he jumped violently, as he suddenly became aware that someone was looking over his shoulder.

"Why don't you come upstairs?" she said. "There's a fire upstairs."

"Blimey, you gave me a start," he said. "I never heard you come in."

"Come up by the fire?" she repeated.

"All right, miss. That's very kind of you. I'll just finish this."

He wrote for another ten minutes, and then followed her up to the room with the fourposter. The bed was smoothly made, the fire leaping. "Nice place," he said, with appreciation, looking round. He sat by the fire.

"Wouldn't you like to go to bed?" she asked.

"Well, thanks, miss, but I'm not sleepy. Had a good kip under a hedge this afternoon. I think I'll read for a bit, unless you feel like a chat."

"That was a sonnet you were writing, wasn't it? Why do you write sonnets?"

"I dunno, really. I just took a fancy to. That's why I'm on the roads. I used to be a seaman, radio technician, till I retired and had me own little business. Then I took this fancy to write sonnets and learn languages. Well, after all, you've only got one life, got to please yourself sometimes, haven't you? So my daughter and son-in-law that I lived with, they got fed up and gave me the push."

"Your own daughter turned you out?" she said, shocked.

"You couldn't blame her, lass, with me not bringing in any money. Matter of fact, I've been happier since then than ever in me life. No worries, got my transistor if ever I feel lonely. Like a bit of music?"

He turned a switch and suddenly the room was filled with sweet, orderly sound.

"Good, isn't it? That's Hamburg. Made the set myself."

"But that is a galliard!" she said, her face lighting up. "We used to dance to it. Like this!"

She rose and began turning and gliding before him, holding up her brocade skirts so that the jewels in her buckled shoes glittered in the firelight.

"Brayvo!" he said. "That's as good as Sadlers' Wells!"

"You dance too!" She caught at his hand. "Oh, what a long time it is since I danced!"

"Me, lass? I don't know how. All I ever learned was the two-step."

"I can show you. See how easy it is? The music carries you."

And indeed it did seem that the music was guiding him through the intricate courtly pattern of the dance. He stepped erectly, and his blue eyes shone at her as she moved and dipped, graceful as a ship under full sail. One dance followed another, and yet he was not tired, or conscious of any incongruity in their dancing together. At last the music ended and she swept him a deep curtsey.

"See," she said, "we have danced so long that dawn is breaking. I never thought to dance again."

"So we have. So we have. And yet I don't feel tired at all.

I believe I could walk sixty miles this very minute, and never notice."

He looked out of the window. A wild and ragged dawn was breaking over the wet roofs of the town. Pointed gables gleamed in the first light.

"I'd best be off, I reckon. Thank you kindly for the night's shelter, lass."

"There's a thousand pounds for you if you wait here till eight o'clock," she said. "Stay a bit longer."

He looked blank, then laughed. "What good is a thousand to me? They better build themselves a new school or do something useful with it. No, thank you all the same—I'll be on the move—"

He was halfway along the coast road, where the shingle lay in gleaming heaps, scattered by the receding tide, when he heard her light step behind him.

"I've a mind to come along. Will you let me come with you?" she called.

"And welcome, lass, if you want to."

She tucked her arm through his. "Can we have a bit of music?"

A coastguard, coming out early to survey the storm damage, saw the tramp but not the girl. Till the end of his days he carried a memory of the man with ragged clothes and clear blue eyes, who went free as the air along the battered coast road, stepping out briskly to the music of Mr. William Byrd.

Postman's Knock

It all began when Marilyn, feeling about in the post-office box to make sure her parcel had fallen through, found her hand taken in a warm, firm clasp, and a pair of lips gently, yet ardently pressed against it.

Or, no, it began when Fred Hwfa, pushing his red bike up the hill with two soap coupons addressed to The Lady of the House and a form from the Ministry of Agriculture relating to fowl pest, looked over a wall and saw an enchantingly pretty girl picking rhubarb.

Or perhaps it began when the entire sixth form of St. Imelda's School for Girls, having been to a matinée of his play *Medea*, burst in on the dramatist in his London home just as he was triumphantly hammering down the first two lines of a new tragedy entitled (without any marked originality) *Antigone*.

Really, of course, the whole thing originated with Fred's great-uncle the Nabob and his Arabian jar. The jar was not a particularly large one, but it was rather attractive in appearance, rounded and solid, and made of some blue stone with a faint sheen on it like alabaster. It was too small to be used for pot plants, too large for an ashtray, but Fred kept it on his desk, since it was the only personal possession his great-uncle had left him, apart from a hundred and fifty thousand pounds and the London house. But you cannot classify these as personal bequests, whereas the jar had been specifically mentioned. "All I die possessed of and my blue Arabian jar to my great-nephew Frederick Sebastian Hwfa . . ."

The money was if anything an inconvenience, since, before his plays had become so successful, Fred had achieved a most adequate technique for living on cheese and carrots, which he was perfectly prepared to continue indefinitely. The house was a mausoleum in that part of London which might be called Chutney, falling as it does somewhere between Chelsea and Putney. He felt in duty bound to live in it, and at once fell prey to his admirers.

For by some mysterious spring tide of public opinion, Fred's tragedies had become immensely popular. Glasses of stout, small ports, pints of beer stood untasted on saloon bars, while his heart-broken lines sobbed and muttered out of radio or television sets, and customers listened spellbound.

Poor Fred was shy to the roots of his eyelashes. He detested public notice. He had taken a dive into the font at his christening rather than face the scrutiny of all his aunts, and his behaviour since then had been of a similar pattern, culminating in his deliberate choice of playwriting as a career, for it had never occurred to him that he might become a *successful* playwright.

When the thirty hockey-playing prefects from St. Imelda's burst into his study, he was appalled. He looked round frantically for a means of escape. There was no second door, but his eye lit on the blue jar by his typewriter. Something about it beckoned him—an infinitestimal blue nod passed over its surface—and the next moment, neat as ninepence, he had climbed inside it, and the autograph hunters were looking about the room in perplexed disappointment.

"I could have sworn I saw him over Rosalie's shoulder—"

"*I* thought he was here—"

"If he's not in this room, ladies, then he's out," said the butler, who, having been overborne by the first assault wave, was now making a comeback. And he marshalled them back down the stairs past the Nabob's engravings of the Acropolis under fire.

Presently Fred raised a cautious eye above the rim of the jar and, finding peace restored, clambered happily out to immerse himself once more in Antigone's troubles. That was a most useful legacy of Uncle Swithin's, he reflected; hitherto he had not appreciated its worth, but from now on he was never going to be parted from it by more than three feet.

He found it so useful, indeed, and spent so much time in it dodging his fans that at last his doctor, surveying him sternly, told him that his lungs would atrophy from lack of use unless he found some outdoor occupation.

It was at this point that Fred thankfully gave up his uncle's house and took a job as postman in a remote and backward district where it was to be hoped that no one would have heard of him. A postman's life, he thought, should be ideal, since it was solitary, healthy, and contained plenty of opportunity for those long, brooding walks during which the creative spirit begins to work and ferment. Moreover postmen are seldom required to communicate with their fellow men save by the medium of raps on doors.

Naturally, though, he took his jar with him.

One of the first things he did, and this was completely outside the programme he had laid down for himself, was to fall in love.

In the country, of course, people do not take letters for granted as city dwellers do. They know that writing a letter entails coming in out of the garden, finding the ink in its nest among bast and seed potatoes, and a pen from the drawer under the chick incubators; then paper has to be procured, and finally the letter has to be taken six miles to the post and then carried up hill and down dale, through rain and shine, by the devoted postman. So Fred soon found that he was being handed clutches of eggs and vegetable marrows in exchange for pools coupons and poultry-feed advertisements.

Next he began to find his mind freewheeling ahead of him to the white cottage by the millpool and his gifts of rhubarb from Marilyn Gillan.

There was nothing out of the common about Marilyn, save that she was pretty as a sea pink, curvilinear as a seashell, and had a very poor memory for faces, particularly male faces. Psychologists could have traced this to the fact that Marilyn was the elder sister of identical triplet brothers. Owing to the early death of her mother, she had had the care of the triplets, Matthew, Mark, and Luke, since she was twelve years old. As their faces were indistinguishable, she had formed the habit of identifying them by their legs, since Matthew's were bandy, Mark's knock-kneed, and Luke's spindly as ball-point pens. This worked all right until they went into long trousers; after that Marilyn gave up trying to tell them apart. In the meantime she had lost the knack of distinguishing faces and had to rely on her memory for legs, which, when confronted by the trousered male sex, was little help to her.

She had worked in London up to the time when her firm was taken over by new management. Marilyn tried in vain to memorise the faces of the new directors so that she could be civil to them when she met them in the lift. She constantly held doors open for surprised electricians and messengers, but was not sacked until she asked the managing director to whistle her up a taxi.

Much relieved, Marilyn rented a cottage in the wilds and began taking in paying guests, which suited her perfectly. People wrote booking rooms for specific dates, and so, when they arrived, she had no doubt as to who they were. She was so friendly, and her beds were so soft, and her cottage pie so delicious that departing guests invariably booked for the same week the following year, and when they returned, Marilyn, after consulting her booking diary, was able to say, "How nice to see you again, Mr. and Mrs. Hardcastle," without giving away the fact that, to the best of her recollection, she had never seen their faces before.

Somehow when Fred first saw her over the wall, she reminded him of his jar; perhaps it was the blueness of her eyes or the delicate and yet sturdy curve of the hip on which the basket of rhubarb was poised. There was something both reassuring and tantalising about her appearance, and Fred longed to know her better.

He soon found, however, that she was a puzzle. For instance, the first time he knocked on her door with a letter she called out, "Who's there?"

"Fred."

"Fred who?"

"Fred Hwfa."

"Hwfa loaf is better than no bread," said this enigmatic girl (who had acquired some regrettably schoolboyish habits from her brothers).

While Fred stood scratching his head over this, she opened the door fully, noticed his uniform, beamed, said, "You must be the new postman, Fred. Fred any good books lately?" and invited him in for a glass of cherry wine. After that his heart was lost for ever.

When Marilyn learned that he was the author of *Medea, Orion*, and the rest of them, which he was soon tempted to confess, she evinced a becoming respect but did not burst into hysterical fan giggles. Instead she remarked, "Keep Orion the ball," with her disconcerting grin.

But what puzzled Fred most of all was that on the occasions when she met him out of uniform, or in the streets of Poldickery, the market town where postmen were two a penny, she would pass him without a smile or sign of recognition. It was all very mysterious, and added to her elusive charm.

Fred himself was vague and absent enough, in all conscience, for his new play was carrying him along like a velocipede, and he rode on his postman's rounds knee-deep in blank verse, kicking unwanted lines out of the way like dead leaves, and sometimes having to go back miles in order to deliver forgotten letters. On one occasion, indeed, when he knocked at Marilyn's door and she called out her usual "Who's there?" before opening, he was so absorbed that, absently gazing at her hand on the door jamb with its green signet ring, he answered, "Antigone."

There was a baffled silence inside the door, and then Marilyn's voice suggested tentatively, "Antigone rain no more, no more?"

Fred was so bewildered by this gambit that he put her soap coupon back in his satchel and went on his way in perplexity. When Marilyn looked out he had gone round the corner and there was no one in sight.

Ill consequences were to come of this. One of them was that Marilyn had to walk into Poldickery to post six letters accepting bookings (which normally she would have handed to Fred) and a parcel of rhubarb she was sending to her aunt Edith at Skegness. It was while she was reassuring herself about this parcel's safe arrival in the box that she felt the mysterious postal kiss deposited on her hand like a frank, or an impassioned postmark.

Marilyn let out a faint shriek, and her fingers were instantly released. She drew them out and gazed at them wonderingly. Her first notion, that there was a poltergeist in the postbox, was replaced by the correct one, that a postman had been clearing the cage inside at the moment her hand had entered the slot. But—and here Marilyn's heart went pitapat—*which* postman? Was it Fred? For whom, all secretly, she was beginning to feel a melting, burgeoning tenderness, like the upcurling rose-coloured fronds of the rhubarb in her garden? And if it was Fred, had he known it was her hand? It was true that she wore the green signet ring, but had he recognised it?

With unparalleled courage, Marilyn walked into the post office, asked for a packet of stamped postcards, and blushingly glanced about her. To her dismay there were no less than five postmen in the place, sorting mail, emptying sacks, and filling in various kinds of forms. She beat a discomfited retreat. Had one of them been Fred? Impossible to say. All their faces were alike.

Fred, on his side, had been so alarmed at his rash act that he hardly dared lift his eyes to Marilyn's face from then on. When, as he handed her an income-tax return next day, she turned a becoming pink and asked him in for a glass of cherry wine, he murmured that really he must not stop, and went on his way in a sad turmoil. His tragedy about Antigone faltered, lagged, and came to a standstill; he was unable to get his wretched heroine married off to Haemon.

Things had come to a pretty pass.

Marilyn, however, was not lacking in energy and resolution. She took to walking into Poldickery every day and always posted her letters at the time when a postman cleared the mailbox. Twice more her fingers were kissed in its discreet depth. There must, she thought, be *some* way by which she could discover the identity of her mail admirer; could she slip a noose over the hand, fasten it to a nearby tree, and then dart into the post office while he stood captive?

She shrank, though, from the publicity and excitement this course would arouse; besides, even then, with her lover on a string, how would she be able to discover, without asking him straight out, and thus revealing her disability, whether he was indeed Fred? The only way to be sure of Fred's identity was to encounter him on his regular round.

Then the solution came to her—simple, masterly, leaving no room for doubt on either side.

Next day she loosened her signet ring with a little soap, so that it would glide off easily, and when she posted her letters and the kiss was printed on her palm, she slid off the ring with her thumb and little finger (this was not easy, but she had devoted much practice to it) and deposited it, gently and confidingly, in the hand that held hers. Then, palpitating, she fled away. What if her admirer was not Fred? What if some total stranger misconstrued her gesture and began to pursue her? She would have lost her precious ring in vain, and be subjected to a lot of inconvenience, too.

Next day at post time she could hardly bear her anxiety. She was making rhubarb jam to distract her mind, and the whole cottage was full of the sweet, hot, amorous fragrance of boiling fruit and sugar.

A knock sounded on the door.

"Wh—who's there?" Marilyn murmured in trembling tones.

"Fred!" came the answer—ringing, confident, joyful. Her heart leapt.

"Bring the letters in?" she called. "My hands are all jammy."

He opened the door and came in. When she looked at his face, and then at his hand, Marilyn's doubts were all resolved. His face was ablaze with happiness; his hand, carrying a picture postcard from Skegness, bore her ring. He laid the postcard on the table, gently took the jammy spoon from her hand, and folded her in the embrace that had been waiting for so long.

Hours seemed to pass; the jam boiled over; Antigone sat on her funeral pyre unregarded; the afternoon postal collections were grievously late, and still these lovers remained as if fused together.

"My Andromeda, my Hebe, my Deianeira! Marry me! Be the postmistress of my heart!"

"Oh, Fred," Marilyn whispered, overcome. Then she became practical. "Promise me that you will never, never take that ring off your little finger."

"It needed no asking, my angel."

Thus, after a slight superficial scrutiny, Marilyn was able

to recognise her lover when she met him in the streets of Poldickery, and ran no risk of lavishing her embraces on no doubt equally deserving but less familiar postmen. By the winter, with its hazard of gloves, they would have been safely married for some time and she might have discovered some other landmark by which to recognise him; in any case, if you cut your husband in the street, the situation is not so desperate.

It was agreed that they should continue to live in the mill cottage. Fred endowed Marilyn with his hundred and fifty thousand, to buy a few more articles of furniture. He moved in his own possessions, which consisted of various manuscripts, a few dozen reams of foolscap paper, and his great-uncle's jar. Basking in the society of the delicious Marilyn, he felt less and less need for the reassurance of the jar, but, still it might come in useful, and it looked pleasing on the mantelpiece of the blue-and-white kitchen.

Marilyn would no longer take in paying guests; financially there was now no need for it, and she decided that she would feel more secure—and there would be no possible chance of mistake—if Fred was the only man about the house.

They were married, and who shall speak of the raptures of the wedding night of Fred Hwfa and his bride? Suffice it to say that when Fred woke at seven next morning, his mind was a tumbling, inspired ferment of blank verse and love, Antigone, funeral pyres, Haemon, Marilyn, rhubarb, and rings. His first impulse was to leap out and grab his pen and some paper; his second, more decisive impulse was to wake his sleeping love.

He tapped lightly on her half-averted cheek, and she smiled in her sleep and began to turn to him.

"Who's there?" she said.

Alas for poor Fred, all bemused with love! He answered absently, "Haemon," and Marilyn shot up in the bed, gave him one startled glance, and shrieked, "Haemon? I didn't marry *you*!"

Fred gazed at her, too dumfounded to speak.

"How dare you lie there in my bed, stroking my collarbone?" she stormed. "Leave my room at once!"

Fred, hungry, confused, at a loss, and wearing the less operative half of a pyjama suit, felt in no case to argue. He crept mournfully down the stairs, and, finding the world altogether too complicated for him, climbed into his jar. There, being supplied with enough raw material for at least five acts, he curled up and sank into a trance of composition.

Weeks passed. Poor Marilyn was in despair. She searched in vain for her bridegroom; she haunted the post office, she scrutinised every male hand. No ring to be seen.

Her Aunt Edith in Skegness, finding Marilyn's letters more and more dejected, and the parcels of rhubarb becoming very inferior in quality, came down on a visit to see what ailed her niece.

The loss of a new husband seemed light in Aunt Edith's eyes when set against the background of a hundred and fifty thousand pounds; being a managing woman herself, she decided that plenty of work was all that was needed to set Marilyn to rights, and she encouraged her niece to begin bottling rhubarb. Bottle after bottle, jar after jar, they indefatigably filled with pink and pearly segments, until the shelves in the storeroom resembled some museum of marine monstrosities. But still Marilyn drooped and pined, and Aunt Edith was not satisfied.

"We must bottle more," she declared. "There is still plenty of rhubarb."

"No jars left," sighed Marilyn, for the very thought of rhubarb was linked in her mind with that of Fred.

"Three pickle bottles, a ginger jar, and that thing on the mantelpiece," announced Aunt Edith after a roundup of the house. "That will be sufficient for this small bundle of rhubarb, at all events."

"Fred's jar! I couldn't use that!"

"Nonsense," Aunt Edith said masterfully. "Why ever not? He left you flat; at least you can make some use of the few odds and ends he brought you. Take down the jar; it will hold quite a nice lot of rhubarb." And she stirred her boiling brew.

Marilyn took down the jar, but her hand shook as she thought of her wandering Fred, and she knocked it against the table edge. A surprised voice from inside the jar called out, "Who's there?"

Hardly daring to believe her ears, she whispered, "M-Marilyn!"

Among the other fruits of Fred's meditations in the jar was a solution to Marilyn's puzzling responses to the question "Who's there?"

Now, triumphantly, he remarked,

> "*Marilyn, Marilyn, shall I live now,*
> *Under the blossom that hangs on the bough,*"

and stepping out of the jar, he took his bride in his arms.

Aunt Edith, unaccustomed to sudden and inexplicable appearances of young men in the less operative halves of pyjama suits, screamed and went hastily out into the garden to pick more rhubarb.

"Fred!" Marilyn murmured (having identified him by the ring). "Darling, where have you been all this time?"

"In the jar, of course," he said. "You just try it!" And he kissed her again, picked her up, and climbed back into the jar with her.

They lived happily ever after.

As Gay as Cheese

Mr. Pol, the barber, always wore white overalls. He must have had at least six pairs, for every day he was snowy white and freshly starched as a marguerite, his blue eyes, red face and bulbous nose appearing incongruously over the top of the bib. His shop looked like, and was, a kitchen, roughly adapted to barbering, with a mirror, basin, and some pictures of beautiful girls on the whitewashed walls. It was a long narrow crack of a room with the copper at one end and a tottering flight of steps at the other, leading down to the street; customers waiting their turn mostly sat on the steps in the sun, risking piles and reading *Men Only*.

Mr. Pol rented his upstairs room to an artist, and in the summertime when the customers had been shaved or trimmed, they sometimes went on up the stairs and bought a view of the harbour, water or oil, or a nice still life. The artist had an unlimited supply of these, which he whipped out with the dexterity of a card sharper.

Both men loved their professions. When the artist was not painting fourteen by ten inch squares for the trippers, he was engaged on huge, complicated panels of mermaids, sharks, all mixed up with skulls, roses, and cabbages, while Mr. Pol hung over the heads of his customers as if he would have liked to gild them.

"Ah, I'm as gay as cheese this morning," he used to say,

bustling into his kitchen with a long, gnomish look at the first head of hair waiting to be shorn. "I'll smarten you up till you're like a new button mushroom."

"Now I'm as bright as a pearl," he would exclaim when the long rays of the early sun felt their way back to the copper with an underwater glimmer.

When Mr. Pol laid hands on a customer's head he knew more about that man than his mother did at birth, or his sweetheart or confessor—not only his past misdeeds but his future ones, what he had had for breakfast and would have for supper, the name of his dog and the day of his death. This should have made Mr. Pol sad or cynical, but it did not. He remained impervious to his portentous gift. Perhaps this was because the destinies of the inhabitants of a small Cornish town contained nothing very startling, and Mr. Pol's divinings seldom soared higher or lower than a double twenty or a sprained ankle.

He never cut his own hair, and had no need to, for he was as bald as an egg.

"It was my own hair falling out that started me thinking on the matter," he told the artist. "All a man's nature comes out in the way his hair grows. It's like a river—watch the currents and you can tell what it's come through, what sort of fish are in it, how fast it's running, how far to the sea."

The artist grunted. He was squatting on the floor, stretching a canvas, and made no reply. He was a taciturn man, who despised the trippers for buying his pink-and-green views.

Mr. Pol looked down at the top of his head and suddenly gave it an affectionate, rumpling pat, as one might to a large woolly dog.

"Ah, that's a nice head of hair. It's a shame you won't let me get at it."

"And have you knowing when I'm going to eat my last bite of bacon? Not likely."

"I wouldn't tell you, my handsome!" said Mr. Pol, very shocked. "I'm not one to go measuring people for their coffins before they're ready to step in. I'm as close as a false tooth. There's Sam now, off his lorry, the old ruin; I could tell a thing or two about him, but do I?"

He stumped off down the stairs, letting out a snatch of hymn in his powerful baritone.

"And there's some say," he went on, as he sculpted with his shears round the driver's wicked grey head, "that you can grow turnips from carrot seeds under the right moon. Who'd want to do that, I ask you?"

"Shorter round the ears," grumbled Sam, scowling down into the enamel basin.

When the night train from Paddington began to draw down the narrow valley towards the sea town, Brian and Fanny Dexter stood up stiffly from the seats where they had slept and started moving their luggage about. Brian was surly and silent, only remarking that it was damned cold and he hoped he could get a shave and a cup of coffee. Fanny glanced doubtfully at her reflection in the little greenish mirror. A white face and narrow eyes, brilliant from lack of sleep, glanced back at her.

"It's be fine later," she said hopefully. Brian pulled on a sweater without comment. He looked rough but expensive, like a suede shoe. His thick light hair was beginning to grey, but hardly showed it.

"Lady Ward and Penelope said they'd be getting to Pengelly this week," Brian observed. "We might walk along the cliff path later on and see if they've arrived yet. We can do with some exercise to warm us and they'll be expecting us to call."

"I must do my shopping first. It's early closing, and there's all the food to lay in."

Brian shot her an angry look, and she was reminded that although the ice of their marriage seemed at the moment to be bearing, nevertheless there were frightening depths beneath and it was best not to loiter in doubtful spots.

"It won't take long," she said hurriedly.

"It was just an idea," Brian muttered, bundling up a camelhair overcoat. "Here we are, thank God."

It was still only nine in the morning. The town was grey and forbidding, tilted steeply down to a white sea. The fleet was out; the streets smelt of fish and emptiness. After they had had coffee Brian announced that he was going to get his shave.

"I'll do my shopping and meet you," suggested Fanny.

"No you bloody well won't, or you'll wander off for hours and I shall have to walk half over the town looking for you," snapped Brian. "You could do with a haircut yourself; you look like a Scotch terrier."

"All right."

She threaded her way after him between the empty tables of the café and across the road into Mr. Pol's shop. Mr. Pol was carefully rearranging his tattered magazines.

"Good morning, my handsome," he cautiously greeted Fanny's jeans and sweater and Eton crop, assessing her as a summer visitor.

"Can you give me a shave and my wife a haircut please?" cut in Brian briskly.

Mr. Pol looked from one to the other of them.

"I'll just put the kettle on for the shave, sir," he answered, moving leisurely to the inner room, "and then I'll trim the young lady, if you'd like to take a seat in the meanwhile."

Brian preferred to stroll back and lean against the doorpost with his hands in his pockets, while Mr. Pol wreathed Fanny's neck in a spotless towel. Her dark head, narrow as a boy's, was bent forward, and he looked benignly at the swirl of glossy hair, flicked a comb through it, and turned her head gently with the palms of his hands.

As he did so, a shudder like an electric shock ran through him and he started back, the comb between his thumb and forefinger jerking upward like a diviner's rod. Neither of the other two noticed; Brian was looking out into the street and Fanny had her eyes on her hands, which were locked together with white knuckles across a fold of the towel.

After a moment Mr. Pol gingerly replaced his palms on the sides of her head with a pretence of smoothing the downy hair above the ears, and again the shock ran through him. He looked into the mirror, almost expecting to see fish swimming and seaweed floating around her. Death by drowning, and so soon; he could smell salt water and see her thin arm stretch sideways in the wave.

"Don't waste too much time on her," said Brian looking at his watch. "She doesn't mind what she looks like."

Fanny glanced up and met Mr. Pol's eyes in the glass. There was such a terrified appeal in her look that his hands closed instinctively on her shoulders and his lips shaped to form the words, "There, there, my handsome. Never mind," before he saw that her appeal was directed, not to him, but to her own reflection's pathetic power to please.

"That's lovely," she said to Mr. Pol with a faint smile, and stood up, shaking the glossy dark tufts off her. She sat on one of his chairs, looking at a magazine, while Brian took her place and Mr. Pol fetched his steaming kettle.

"You're visiting the town?" Mr. Pol asked as he rubbed up the lather on his brush. He felt the need for talk.

"Just come off the night train; we're staying here, yes," Brian said curtly.

"It's a pretty place," Mr. Pol remarked. "Plenty of grand walks if you're young and active."

"We're going along to Pengelly by the cliff path this morning," said Brian.

"Oh, but I thought you only said we *might*—" Fanny began incautiously, and then bit off her words.

Brian shot her a look of such hatred that even Mr. Pol caught it, and scuttled into the next room for another razor.

"For Christ's sake, *will* you stop being so damned negative," Brian muttered to her furiously.

"But the groceries—"

"Oh, to hell with the groceries. We'll eat out. Lady Ward and Penelope will think it most peculiar if we don't call—they know we're here. I suppose you want to throw away a valuable social contact for the sake of a couple of ounces of tea. I can't think why you need to do this perpetual shopping—Penelope never does."

"I only thought—"

"Never mind what you thought."

Mr. Pol came back and finished the shave.

"That's a nice head of hair, sir," he said, running his hands over it professionally. "Do you want a trim at all?"

"No, thanks," replied Brian abruptly. "Chap in the Burlington Arcade always does it for me. Anything wrong?"

Mr. Pol was staring at the ceiling above Brian's head in a puzzled way.

"No—no, sir, nothing. Nothing at all. I thought for a moment

I saw a bit of rope hanging down, but it must have been fancy." Nevertheless, Mr. Pol passed his hand once more above Brian's head with the gesture of someone brushing away cobwebs.

"Will that be all? Thank you, sir. Mind how you go on that path to Pengelly. 'Tis always slippery after the rain and we've had one or two falls of rock this summer; all this damp weather loosens them up."

"We'll be all right, thanks," said Brian, who had been walking out of the door without listening to what Mr. Pol was saying. "Come on, Fanny." He swung up the street with Fanny almost running behind him.

"Have they gone? Damnation, I thought I could sell them a view of the cliffs," said the artist, coming in with a little canvas. "Hullo, something the matter?"

For the barber was standing outside his door and staring in indecision and distress after the two figures, now just taking the turning up to the cliff path.

"No," he said at last, turning heavily back and picking up his broom. "No, I'm as gay as cheese."

And he began sweeping up the feathery tufts of dark hair from his stone floor.

Furry Night

THE deserted aisles of the National Museum of Dramatic Art lay very, very still in the blue autumn twilight. Not a whisper of wind stirred the folds of Irving's purple cloak; Ellen Terry's ostrich fan was smooth and unruffled; the blue-black gleaming breastplate that Sir Murdoch Meredith, founder of the museum, had worn as Macbeth held its reflections as quietly as a cottage kettle.

And yet, despite this hush, there was an air of strain, of expectancy, along the narrow coconut-matted galleries between the glass cases: a tension suggesting that some crisis had taken or was about to take place.

In the total stillness a listener might have imagined that he heard, ever so faintly, the patter of stealthy feet far away among the exhibits.

Two men, standing in the shadow of the Garrick showcase, were talking in low voices.

"This is where it happened," said the elder, white-haired man.

He picked up a splinter of broken glass, frowned at it, and dropped it into a litter bin. The glass had been removed from the front of the case, and some black tights and gilt medals hung exposed to the evening air.

"We managed to hush it up. The hospital and ambulance men will be discreet, of course. Nobody else was there, luckily. Only the Bishop was worried."

"I should think so," the younger man said. "It's enough to make anybody anxious."

"No, I mean he was *worried.* Hush," the white-haired man whispered, "here comes Sir Murdoch."

The distant susurration had intensified into soft, pacing footsteps. The two men, without a word, stepped farther back in the shadow until they were out of sight. A figure appeared at the end of the aisle and moved forward until it stood beneath the portrait of Edmund Kean as Shylock. The picture, in its deep frame, was nothing but a square of dark against the wall.

Although they were expecting it, both men jumped when the haunted voice began to speak.

"*You may as well use question with the wolf*
Why he hath made the ewe bleat for the lamb. . . ."

A sleeve of one of the watchers brushed against the wall, the lightest possible touch, but Sir Murdoch swung round sharply, his head outthrust, teeth bared. They held their breath, and after a moment he turned back to the picture.

"*Thy currish spirit*
Govern'd a wolf, who, hang'd for human slaughter
Even from the gallows did his fell soul fleet. . . ."

He paused, with a hand pressed to his forehead, and then leaned forward and hissed,

"*Thy desires*
Are wolvish, bloody, starv'd, and ravenous!"

His head sank on his chest. His voice ceased. He brooded for a moment, and then resumed his pacing and soon passed out of sight. They heard the steps go lightly down the stairs, and presently the whine of the revolving door.

After a prudent interval the two others emerged from their hiding place, left the gallery, and went out to a car that was waiting for them in Great Smith Street.

"I wanted you to see that, Peachtree," said the elder man, "to give you some idea of what you are taking on. Candidly, as far as experience goes, I hardly feel you are qualified for the job, but you are young and tough and have presence of mind; most important of all, Sir Murdoch seems to have taken a fancy to you. You will have to keep an unobtrusive eye on him every minute of the day; your job is a combination of secretary, companion, and resident psychiatrist. I have written to Dr. Defoe, the local GP at Polgrue. He is old, but you will find him full of practical sense. Take his advice . . . I think you said you were brought up in Australia?"

"Yes," Ian Peachtree said. "I only came to this country six months ago."

"Ah, so you missed seeing Sir Murdoch act."

"Was he so very wonderful?"

"He made the comedies too macabre," said Lord Hawick, considering, "but in the tragedies there was no one to touch him. His Macbeth was something to make you shudder. When he said,

> '*Alarum'd by his sentinel, the wolf,*
> *Whose howl's his watch, thus with his stealthy pace,*
> *With Tarquin's ravishing strides, towards his design*
> *Moves like a ghost,*'

he used to take two or three stealthy steps across the stage, and you could literally see the grey fur rise on his hackles, the lips draw back from the fangs, the yellow eyes begin to gleam. It made a cold chill run down your spine. As Shylock and Caesar and Timon he was unrivalled. Othello and Antony he never touched, but his Iago was a masterpiece of villainy."

"Why did he give it up? He can't be much over fifty."

"As with other sufferers from lycanthropy," said Lord Hawick, "Sir Murdoch has an ungovernable temper. Whenever he flew into a rage it brought on an attack. They grew more and more frequent. A clumsy stagehand, a missed cue might set him off; he'd begin to shake with rage and the terrifying change would take place.

"On stage it wasn't so bad; he had his audiences completely hypnotised and they easily accepted a grey-furred Iago padding across the stage with the handkerchief in his mouth. But off stage it was less easy; the claims for mauling and worrying were beginning to mount up; Equity objected. So he retired, and, for some time, founding the museum absorbed him. But now it's finished; his temper is becoming uncertain again. This afternoon, as you know, he pounced on the Bishop for innocently remarking that Garrick's Hamlet was the world's greatest piece of acting."

"How do you deal with the attacks? What's the treatment?"

"Wolfsbane. Two or three drops given in a powerful sedative will restore him for the time. Of course, administering it is the problem, as you can imagine. I only hope the surroundings in Cornwall will be sufficiently peaceful so that he is not provoked. It's a pity he never married; a woman's influence would be beneficial."

"Why didn't he?"

"Jilted when he was thirty. Never looked at another woman. Some girl down at Polgrue, near his home. It was a real slap in the face; she wrote two days before the wedding saying she couldn't stand his temper. That began it all. This will be the first time he's been back there. Well, here we are," said Lord Hawick, glancing out at his Harley Street doorstep. "Come in and I'll give you the wolfsbane prescription."

The eminent consultant courteously held the door for his young colleague.

The journey to Cornwall was uneventful. Dr. Peachtree drove his distinguished patient, glancing at him from time to time with mingled awe and affection. Would the harassing crawl down the A30, the jam in Exeter, the flat tyre on Dartmoor, bring on an attack? Would he be able to cope if they did? But the handsome profile remained unchanged, the golden eyes in their deep sockets stayed the eyes of a man, not those of a wolf, and Sir Murdoch talked entertainingly, not at all discomposed by the delays. Ian was fascinated by his tales of the theatre.

There was only one anxious moment, when they reached the borders of Polgrue Chase. Sir Murdoch glanced angrily at his neglected coverts, where the brambles grew long and wild.

"Wait till I see that agent," he muttered, and then, half to himself, " 'O, thou wilt be a wilderness again,/Peopled with wolves.' "

Ian devoutly hoped that the agent would have a good excuse.

But the Hall, hideous Victorian-Gothic barrack though it was, they found gay with lights and warm with welcome. The old housekeeper wept over Sir Murdoch, bottles were uncorked, the table shone with ancestral silver. Ian began to feel less apprehensive.

After dinner they moved outside with their nuts and wine to sit in the light that streamed over the terrace from the dining-room French windows. A great walnut tree hung shadowy above them; its golden, aromatic leaves littered the flagstones at their feet.

"This place has a healing air," Sir Murdoch said. "I should have come here sooner." Suddenly he stiffened. "Hudson! Who are those?"

Far across the park, almost out of sight in the dusk, figures were flitting among the trees.

"Eh," said the housekeeper comfortably, "they're none but the lads, Sir Murdoch, practising for the Furry Race. Don't you worrit about them. They won't do no harm."

"On my land?" Sir Murdoch said. "Running across my land?"

Ian saw with a sinking heart that his eyes were turning to gleaming yellow slits, his hands were stiffening and curling. Would the housekeeper mind? Did she know her master was subject to these attacks? He felt in his pocket for the little ampoules of wolfsbane, the hypodermic syringe.

There came an interruption. A girl's clear voice was heard singing:

"*Now the hungry lion roars,*
And the wolf behowls the moon—"

"It's Miss Clarissa," said the housekeeper with relief.

A slender figure swung round the corner of the terrace and came towards them.

"Sir Murdoch? How do you do? I'm Clarissa Defoe. My father sent me up to pay his respects. He would have come himself, but he was called out on a case. Isn't it a gorgeous night?"

Sitting down beside them, she chatted amusingly and easily, while Ian observed with astonished delight that his employer's hands were unclenching and his eyes were becoming their normal shape again. If this girl was able to soothe Sir Murdoch without recourse to wolfsbane, they must see a lot of her.

But when Sir Murdoch remarked that the evening was becoming chilly and proposed that they go indoors, Ian's embryonic plan received a jolt. He was a tough and friendly young man who had never taken a great deal of interest in girls; the first sight, in lamplight, of Clarissa Defoe's wild beauty came on him with a shattering impact. Could he expose her to danger without warning her?

More and more enslaved, he sat gazing as Clarissa played and sang Ariel's songs. Sir Murdoch seemed completely charmed and relaxed. When Clarissa left, he let Ian persuade him to bed without the topic of the Furry Race coming up again.

Next morning, however, when Ian went down to the village for a consultation with cheerful, shrewd-eyed old Dr. Defoe, he asked about it.

"Heh," said the doctor. "The Furry Race? My daughter revived it five years ago. There's two villages, ye see, Polgrue, and Lostmid, and there's this ball, what they call the Furry Ball. It's not furry; it's made of applewood with a silver band round the middle, and on the band is written,

Fro Lostmid Parish iff I goe
Heddes will be broke and bloode will flowe.

"The ball is kept in Lostmid, and on the day of the race one of the Polgrue lads has to sneak in and take it and get it over the parish boundary before anybody stops him. Nobody's succeeded in doing it yet. But why do you ask?"

Ian explained about the scene the night before.

"Eh, I see; that's awkward. You're afraid it may bring on an attack if he sees them crossing his land? Trouble is, that's the quickest shortcut over the parish boundary."

"If your daughter withdrew her support, would the race be abandoned?"

"My dear feller, she'd never do that. She's mad about it. She's a bit of a tomboy, Clarissa, and the roughhousing amuses her—always is plenty of horseplay, even though they don't get the ball over the boundary. If her mother were still alive now . . .

Bless my soul!" the old doctor burst out, looking troubled, "I wish Meredith had never come back to these parts, that I do. You can speak with Clarissa about it, but I doubt you'll not persuade her. She's out looking over the course now."

The two villages of Lostmid and Polgrue lay in deep adjacent glens, and Polgrue Chase ended on the stretch of high moorland that ran between them. There was a crossroads and a telephone box, used by both villages. A spinney of wind-bitten beeches stood in one angle of the cross, and Clarissa was thoughtfully surveying this terrain. Ian joined her, turning to look back towards the Hall and noticing with relief that Sir Murdoch was still, as he had been left, placidly knocking a ball round his private golf course.

It was a stormy, shining day. Ian saw that Clarissa's hair was exactly the colour of the sea-browned beech leaves and that the strange angles of her face were emphasised by the wild shafts of sunlight glancing through the trees.

He put his difficulties to her.

"Oh dear," she said, wrinkling her brow. "How unfortunate. The boys are so keen on the race. I don't think they'd ever give it up."

"Couldn't they go some other way?"

"But this is the only possible way, don't you see? In the old days, of course, all this used to be common land."

"Do you know who the runner is going to be—the boy with the ball?" Ian asked, wondering if a sufficiently heavy bribe would persuade him to take a longer way round.

But Clarissa smiled, with innocent topaz eyes. "My dear, that's never decided until the very *last* minute. So that the Lostmidians don't know who's going to dash in and snatch the ball. But I'll tell you what we *can* do—we can arrange for the race to take place at night, so that Sir Murdoch won't be worried by the spectacle. Yes, that's an excellent idea; in fact, it will make it far more exciting. It's next Thursday, you know."

Ian was not at all sure that he approved of this idea, but just then he noticed Sir Murdoch having difficulties in a bunker. A good deal of sand was flying about, and his employer's face was becoming a dangerous dusky red. " 'Here, in the sands,/Thee I'll rake up,' " he was muttering angrily, and something about murderous lechers.

Ian ran down to him and suggested that it was time for a glass of beer, waving to Clarissa as he did so. Sir Murdoch noticed her and was instantly mollified. He invited her to join them.

Ian, by now head over heels in love, was torn between his professional duty, which could not help pointing out to him how beneficial Clarissa's company was for his patient, and a strong personal feeling that the elderly wolfish baronet was not at all suitable company for Clarissa. Worse, he suspected that she guessed his anxiety and was laughing at it.

The week passed peacefully enough. Sir Murdoch summoned the chairmen of the two parish councils and told them that any trespass over his land on the day of the Furry Race would be punished with the utmost rigour. They listened with blank faces. He also ordered man traps and spring guns from the Dominion and Colonial Stores, but to Ian's relief it seemed highly unlikely that these would arrive in time.

Clarissa dropped in frequently. Her playing and singing seemed to have as soothing an effect on Sir Murdoch as the songs of the harpist David on touchy old Saul, but Ian had the persistent feeling that some peril threatened from her presence.

On Furry Day she did not appear. Sir Murdoch spent most of the day pacing—loping was really the word for it, Ian thought—distrustfully among his far spinneys, but no trespasser moved in the bracken and dying leaves. Towards evening a fidgety scuffling wind sprang up, and Ian persuaded his employer indoors.

"No one will come, Sir Murdoch, I'm sure. Your notices have scared them off. They'll have gone another way." He wished he really did feel sure of it. He found a performance of *Caesar and Cleopatra* on TV and switched it on, but Shaw seemed to make Sir Murdoch impatient. Presently he got up, began to pace about, and turned it off, muttering,

> "*And why should Caesar be a tyrant, then?*
> *Poor man! I know he would not be a wolf!*"

He swung round on Ian. "Did I do wrong to shut them off my land?"

"Well—" Ian was temporising when there came an outburst of explosions from Lostmid, hidden in the valley, and a dozen rockets soared into the sky beyond the windows.

"That means someone's taken the Furry Ball," said Hudson, coming in with the decanter of sherry. "Been long enough about it, seemingly."

Sir Murdoch's expression changed completely. One stride took him to the French window. He opened it and went streaking across the park. Ian bolted after him.

"Stop! Sir Murdoch, stop!"

Sir Murdoch turned an almost unrecognisable face and hissed, " 'Wake not a sleeping wolf!' " He kept on his way, with Ian stubbornly in pursuit. They came out by the crossroads and, looking down to Lostmid, saw that it was a circus of wandering lights, clustering, darting this way and that.

"They've lost him," Ian muttered. "No, there he goes!"

One of the lights broke off at a tangent and moved away down the valley, then turned and came straight for them diagonally across the hillside.

"I'll have to go and warn him off," Ian thought. "Can't let him run straight into trouble." He ran downhill towards the approaching light. Sir Murdoch stole back into the shade of the spinney. Nothing of him was visible but two golden, glowing eye points.

It was at this moment that Clarissa, having established her red-herring diversion by sending a boy with a torch across the hillside, ran swiftly and silently up the steep road towards the sign-post. She wore trousers and a dark sweater and was clutching the Furry Ball in her hand.

Sir Murdoch heard the pit-pat of approaching footsteps, waited for his moment, and sprang.

It was the thick fisherman's-knit jersey with its roll collar that saved her. They rolled over and over, girl and wolf entangled, and then she caught him a blow on the jaw with the heavy applewood ball, dropped it, scrambled free, and was away. She did not dare look back. She had a remarkable turn of speed, but the wolf was overtaking her. She hurled herself into the telephone box and let the door clang to behind her.

The wolf arrived a second later; she heard the impact as the grey, sinewy body struck the door, saw the gleam of teeth through the glass. Methodically, though with shaking hands, she turned to dial.

Meanwhile Ian had met the red-herring boy just as his triumphant pursuers caught up with him.

"You mustn't go that way!" Ian gasped. "Sir Murdoch's waiting up there and he's out for blood."

"Give over that thurr ball," yelled the Lostmidians.

" 'Tisn't on me," the boy yelled back, regardless of the fact that he was being pulled limb from limb. "Caught ye properly, me fine fules. 'Tis Miss Clarissa's got it, and she'm gone backaway."

"*What?*"

Ian waited for no more. He left them to their battle, in which some Polgrue reinforcements were now joining, and bounded back up the murderous ascent to where he had left Sir Murdoch.

The scene at the telephone box was brilliantly lit by the overhead light. Clarissa had finished her call and was watching with detached interest as the infuriated wolf threw himself repeatedly against the door.

It is not easy to address your employer in such circumstances. Ian chose a low, controlled, but vibrant tone.

"Down, Sir Murdoch," he said. "Down, sir! Heel!"

Sir Murdoch turned on him a look of golden, thunderous wrath. He was really a fine spectacle, with his eyes flashing, and great ruff raised in rage. He must have weighed all of a hundred and thirty pounds. Ian thought he might be a timber wolf, but was not certain. He pulled the ampoule from his pocket, charged the syringe, and made a cautious approach. Instantly Sir Murdoch flew at him. With a feint like a bullfighter's, Ian dodged round the call box.

"Olé," Clarissa shouted approvingly, opening the door a crack. Sir Murdoch instantly turned and battered it again.

" 'Avaunt, thou damnéd door-keeper!' " shouted Ian. The result was electrifying. The wolf dropped to the ground as if stunned. Ian seized advantage of the moment to give him his injection, and immediately the wolf shape vanished, dropping off Sir Murdoch like a label off a wet bottle. He gasped, shivered, and shut his eyes.

"Where am I?" he said presently, opening them again. Ian

took his arm, gently led him away from the door, and made him sit on a grassy bank.

"You'll feel better in a minute or two, sir," he said, and, since Shakespeare seemed so efficacious, added, " 'The cure whereof, my lord,/'Tis time must do.' " Sir Murdoch weakly nodded.

Clarissa came out of her refuge. "Are you all right now, Sir Murdoch?" she asked kindly. "Shall I sing you a song?"

"All right, thank you, my dear," he murmured. "What are you doing here?" And he added to himself, "I really must not fly into these rages. I feel quite dizzy."

Ian stepped aside and picked up something that glinted on the ground.

"What's that?" asked Sir Murdoch with awakening interest. "It reminds me— May I see it?"

"Oh, it's my medallion," said Clarissa at the same moment. "It must have come off. . . ." Her voice trailed away. They both watched Sir Murdoch. Deep, fearful shudders were running through him.

"Where did you get this?" he demanded, turning his cavernous eyes on Clarissa. His fingers were rigid, clenched on the tiny silver St. Francis.

"It was my mother's," she said faintly. For the first time she seemed frightened.

"Was her name Louisa?" She nodded. "Then, your father—?"

"Here comes my father now," said Clarissa with relief. The gnarled figure of the doctor was approaching them through the spinney. Sir Murdoch turned on him like a javelin.

" 'O thou foul thief!' " he hissed. "My lost Louisa! 'Stol'n from me and corrupted/By spells and medicines.' "

"Oh, come, come, come," said the doctor equably, never slowing his approach, though he kept a wary eye on Sir Murdoch. "I wouldn't put it quite like that. She came to me. *I* was looking forward to bachelorhood."

" 'For the which I may go the finer, I will live a bachelor,' " murmured Ian calmingly.

"And I'll tell ye this, Sir Murdoch," Dr. Defoe went on, tucking his arm through that of Sir Murdoch like an old friend, "you were well rid of her." He started strolling at a gentle but purposeful pace back towards the Hall, and the baronet went with him doubtfully.

"Why is that?" Already Sir Murdoch sounded half convinced, quiescent.

"Firstly, my dear sir, Temper. Out of this world! Secondly, Macaroni Cheese. Every night till one begged for mercy. Thirdly, Unpunctuality. Fourthly, long, horrifying Dreams, which she insisted on telling at breakfast . . ."

Pursuing this soothing, therapeutic vein, the doctor's voice moved farther away, and the two men were lost in the shadows.

"So that's all right," said Clarissa on a deep breath of relief. "Why, Ian!"

Pent-up agitation was too much for him. He had grabbed her in his arms like a drowning man. "I was sick with fright for you," he muttered, into her hair, her ear, the back of her neck. "I was afraid—oh well, never mind."

"Never mind," she agreed. "Are we going to get married?"

"Of course."

"I ought to find my Furry Ball," she said presently. "They seem to be having a pitched battle down below; there's a good chance of getting it over the boundary while everyone's busy."

"But Sir Murdoch—"

"Father will look after him."

She moved a few steps away and soon found the ball. "Come on; through the wood is quickest. We have to put it on the Polgrue churchyard wall."

No one accosted them as they ran through the wood. Fireworks and shouting in the valley suggested that Lostmid and Polgrue had sunk their differences in happy saturnalia.

"Full surgery tomorrow," remarked Clarissa, tucking the Furry Ball into its niche. "Won't someone be surprised to see this."

When Ian and Clarissa strolled up to the terrace, they found Sir Murdoch and the doctor amiably drinking port. Sir Murdoch looked like a man who had had a festering grief removed from his mind.

"Well," the doctor said cheerfully, "we've cleared up some misunderstandings."

But Sir Murdoch had stood up and gone to meet Clarissa.

" 'As I am a man,' " he said gravely,/" 'I do think this lady/ To be my child.' "

The two pairs of golden eyes met and acknowledged each other.

"That'll be the end of his little trouble, I shouldn't wonder," murmured the doctor. "Specially if she'll live at the Hall and keep an eye on him."

"But she's going to marry me."

"All the better, my dear boy. All the better. And glad I shall be to get rid of her, bless her heart."

Ian looked doubtfully across the terrace at his future father-in-law, but he recalled that wolves are among the most devoted fathers of the animal kingdom. Sir Murdoch was stroking Clarissa's hair with an expression of complete peace and happiness.

Then a thought struck Ian. "If *he's* her father—"

But Dr. Defoe was yawning. "I'm off to bed. Busy day tomorrow." He vanished among the dark trees.

So they were married and lived happily at the Hall. Clarissa's slightest wish was law. She was cherished equally by both father and husband, and if they went out of their way not to cross her in any particular, this was due quite as much to the love they bore her as to their knowledge that they had dangerous material on their hands.

Five Green Moons

THIS small town was of course full of people and, like all such places, so beautiful and so interesting that it would take a lifetime to describe it. But we will pick one particular morning in May when children were at school, and washing was blossoming out on lines, and delivery vans were edging their way from the narrow streets out into the countryside and, generally speaking, in all the town's not very numerous alleys and backyards and shops and houses, life, as vigorous and complex as grass roots, was being lived in the usual way.

Mr. Makins, the bus conductor, was sitting in the small communal courtyard outside his back door smoking a pipe and reading the *Daily Mirror*, since he would not be on duty till twelve. He was soaking his feet, as a precaution against the sudden warm weather, in a polythene bowl of mustard and permanganate, and his solid bulk was comfortably accommodated in an upright canvas deck chair. Sam, the large black Labrador from the Kings', next door, lay beside him, chin on paws, extending a blissful stomach along the warm concrete.

Mrs. Bowling, Rita, from next door on the other side, was doing a little weeding in the centre flowerbed; old blind Mr. Thatcher, next door but one, in Panama and dark glasses, was methodically shaking out his doormat before taking his white stick and tip-tapping through the peaceful town to do some shopping for himself and his granddaughter Lucy, a nurse at the cottage hospital.

That takes care of the externals. And as for what was going on below the surface—Mr. Makins was wondering should he or shouldn't he put on a kettle and make a cup of tea for his wife, Lily, who would soon be back from washing up at The Crown; Sam the Labrador was waiting in warm suspended animation for eleven-year-old Michael to come home from school; Rita Bowling, wan, washed-out, and pretty, was making up her mind to leave her husband, Fred; Mrs. King, who, since the recent death of her husband, had, from unhappiness, been more or less actively unkind to her son, Michael, was reading the day's horoscope in her curtained, fusty, north-facing front room before going to call on the vet; and old Mr. Thatcher was wondering whether Lucy would fancy a nice bit of haddock for supper.

Father Fogarty came up the alley to visit Fred Bowling.

"Morning, Harry. Lovely show of grape hyacinths you've got there," he said, looking admiringly round the little court, which, between walls and concrete paving, was as cosy with flowers as a chintz chair cover. "You can smell them halfway down the alley. Morning, Mrs. Bowling. Is Fred about?"

"Ah, what's the use of speaking to him then, Father?" Rita straightened herself dispiritedly. "You might as well save your bre—"

It was at this moment than an unusual event occurred.

With a brilliant, silent flash—so brilliant, so silent, that it was as if all the light in the world had been sucked in one direction and then blown back again—something came to rest in the middle of the courtyard, crushing to slime, regrettably, a lot of Mr. Makins' grape hyacinths and Mrs. Bowling's narcissi. Three of the four people in the court jumped back instinctively and now stood goggle-eyed, gazing at this strange object which rested in their yard as neatly as a cabbage in a colander.

It was like nothing in the world so much as a duck egg—only, of course, a great deal larger. Higher than Father Fogarty's head, shining, spherical, and slightly translucent, there it stuck among the narcissi, and it was slightly cracked.

"Gor blimey," said Mr. Makins, removing his pipe from his mouth. "Someone's laid an egg. Whatever blessed chick's going to come out of that there?"

"It's a missile!" shrilled Rita. "I bet you anything you like it's got Russians inside it!"

"This is most uncommon," remarked Father Fogarty. He approached the thing gingerly and laid a hand on it. It tipped slightly. "Why, it's quite light. Do you suppose—?"

"Hold on," Harry warned him. "There's someone inside it. You're right, Rita, it's a blooming spaceship."

Sure enough, they could see through the semitransparent skin of the egg that someone was bumping about inside.

"Shall I fetch a hammer?" suggested Harry.

"What's going on, what's going on?" cried old Mr. Thatcher impatiently.

Lil Makins arrived with her shopping bag and let out a little scream. "Oh, Harry! Whatever is it?"

"Wait a minute," said Father Fogarty. "He's coming out."

A tiny biting blade, a kind of circular saw, was cutting a neat division along the line of the crack. As they watched, a section of the egg surface swung back. The knuckles of a hand appeared on the side of the hole. A foot came through, and then a leg. The other leg emerged, followed, with a wriggle, by the torso and head of a young man. He stood up and stared somewhat dazedly at the people confronting him. They stared back.

He was a very thin individual with a shock of light brown hair, an indeterminate nose, and a good-tempered mouth. His eyes, set wide apart, were grey and dispassionate. He had a pair of wings, white, and rather untidy as to the feathers.

"Do you speak English, young man?" said Father Fogarty, obviously feeling that it behoved him to make the first move.

"He must be an angel!" audibly whispered Mrs. Makins to Mrs. Bowling.

"What's going on? What's happened?" asked old Mr. Thatcher irritably.

"Is this the Isle of Albion, sir?" the young man said, addressing himself to Father Fogarty.

"Why, yes—yes, I suppose it is. May one ask where you come from?" The priest achieved a masterly blend of respect, cordiality, and judgement in suspense with these words: if you are an angel, he might have seen saying, I am naturally prepared to extend professional consideration and trade rates, as it were, but although I have a kind heart I am not to be imposed on.

"Mars is my home planet," the young man said diffidently. "But—"

"Mars!" shrieked Mrs. Makins. "He's a Martian!"

"Are there any more of you on the way?" asked Harry, casting a weather eye up to see if other cream-coloured eggs were drifting down out of the blue sky.

"It's a Martian invasion! We're doomed!"

"Belt up, Lil," said Mr. Makins good-naturedly. "They'd send a reconnaissance first, wouldn't they? Well, then, we've just got to discourage this one."

"You are not an angel, young man?"

"You just fly back to Mars and tell them to invade somewhere else. We like our own ways."

"What is it? What *is* it?" snapped Mr. Thatcher.

"It's a Martian invasion," Rita Bowling explained patiently to the irascible old man.

Fred Bowling, roused by the tumult, put his bleary head out of a window and said, "Gawd!"

His wife called up to him, "It's a Martian invasion, Fred!"

The young man from Mars pressed his hands to his forehead. "No, no. You are making a mistake, I assure you," he said earnestly. "I am not invading you and I am not an angel."

"What are you then?"

"My name is Onil. I'm a refugee."

At this moment Police Constable Vyall appeared, taking a shortcut through to the station house. "What's all the ruckus about?" he said. "Strewth! Where did that come from? This is a right of way, I'd have you know. You can't park it here."

"I regret," said the young man faintly. "I am rather exhausted. If you will tell me—"

He looked helplessly round at the ring of simple, wondering, not unfriendly faces watching him, said again, "I'm a refugee," took a staggering step, and fell among what was left of the narcissi.

"Passed out," said Henry. "Better get him to hospital."

"My car's at the end of the alley," said Father Fogarty, "I'll take him. Have you a jacket, Harry, just to cover up the—the wings? We don't want a lot of talk."

"11.09 a.m.," Constable Vyall wrote in his notebook. "Martian and spaceship landed in Viners' Court. Martian removed to hospital."

It was surprising how quickly the townspeople settled to the fact that they had their very own Martian in a side ward at the cottage hospital. (His trouble turned out to be simply a slowness in adjusting to the atmosphere; so long as he had an oxygen mask handy, he was all right.) Naturally there was a stream of visitors both to the hospital and to see the ship, which had to be left in the yard, since it was too large to go through the alley, but it was tacitly and universally agreed that the news should not be allowed to spread outside the town.

"We don't want half the country traipsing here to see him," said Father Fogarty.

"That we don't," agreed Harry Makins.

As Onil had no kinsfolk of his own to visit him, the neighbours took turns bringing him grapes and confiding their troubles. He listened with kindly, dispassionate attention and told them things they hardly knew about themselves.

"Shall I leave Fred or not?" said Rita Bowling.

"You don't really want to. Why not teach him to play chess?"

"What does Lil want for her birthday?" said Harry Makins.

"A pudding basin. One of those red glass ones."

"What shall I get for Lucy's supper?" said old Mr. Thatcher.

"A nice bit of cod and chips from The Red Lion."

"You're putting me out of business," said Father Fogarty.

"I am so happy to be here." The young man Onil looked with love out of his bedroom window at a bit of hedge, all bursting with May buds, and some fat, brown, contented hens.

"Tell me, why did you leave Mars to come to this rather backward little planet?"

"Mars has developed too far," Onil explained. "Nothing remains unknown there. Oh, it is terrible! All we can do is organise each other."

"I can sympathise. That wouldn't do for us down here," said

Father Fogarty, and he rose to go as Nurse Thatcher came in with Onil's lunch on a tray. Young Michael King appeared with a bunch of radishes and his dog, Sam. Boy and dog sat down in a puddle of sunshine on the polished floor.

"Go on telling about your trip," said Michael, and Lucy lingered, dusting the windowsill with a teacloth as she listened.

"Well, space is like a jungle, you know, and each star or planet is a potential Something that might eat you up. . . . I went drifting through the forest, keeping a sharp lookout for a place where people still had time to knit and gossip with their neighbours and read books and sew on buttons and listen to music. . . ."

"No buttons on Mars?"

"Nothing but zips."

"Go on."

"And I saw one or two possibles—yes, there was one nice little planet that I noticed, a long way off, with five green moons and four blue oceans and three extinct volcanoes—"

"And a partridge in a pear tree?" suggested Lucy, sitting on the windowsill so that the sun made a Saturn's ring round her fair hair.

"—but it had no inhabitants, so I thought I'd be too lonely there. And then I saw this one and heard the cuckoos—they don't have any cuckoos on Mars—and I thought, That's the world for me."

"Tell more about the little planet. What was its name?"

"Sirun. It has birds and apple trees, but no people."

"I'll go there when I'm old enough to be a space pilot," said Michael. "Won't we, Sam?" Sam thumped his tail on the floor.

"Time I tidied you up for the doctor," said Lucy, and she took away Onil's tray and straightened up his wings.

Dr. Bentinck was kind, busy, and preoccupied as always. "I think you can soon leave off the oxygen for good. But no violent exercise at first, mind. Thinking of taking a job in the town? Well, be sure it's not too active—librarian, bank clerk, something like that, eh? Nurse Thatcher, can you see where I put my glasses? Ah, thank you, thank you. Good day, young man."

In the evening Fred Bowling came in to play chess. "That Rita," he said. "Honest to God, sometimes I think she'll drive me clean crackers. I swear I don't know sometimes what goes on inside that head of hers."

"Think yourself lucky," said Onil, moving out his queen.

"Eh?"

"Think how much worse it would be if you did know. Why not buy her a record player with your pools winnings?"

"Eh—oh, yes. Forgot I'd told you about that. Yes, come to think, that's not a bad idea, she'd like a player. I've always wanted one too. Then we could listen to records instead of arguing, I suppose. Young Michael's very upset," he went on, hustling a bishop in front of his king.

"Oh, yes?"

"His dog's lost. You know how much store he sets by Sam. That's why he's not come up to see you this evening—he's out on his bike, scouring the place."

"Time you were off, Mr. Bowling," said Night Sister, putting her head round the door.

"Have a heart, Sister! I'm in check! Nurse Thatcher would let me stay."

"Nurse Thatcher spoils this patient."

But even Night Sister was not averse to sitting in the side ward for half an hour and listening to descriptions of washing machines on Mars.

Three days later Onil was allowed out for a brief spell. He strolled through the town to inspect his spaceship, and stopped for a chat with Harry Makins, who was soaking his feet in the yard.

"Getting quite used to it," said Harry, nodding at the bright translucent globe. "Puts me in mind of the Festival of Britain."

Lil brought them a cup of tea, and old Mr. Thatcher pottered by on his way to the shops.

"Don't you have blind people on Mars?" asked Harry, noticing a troubled expression in Onil's eyes as he turned to look after the old man.

"No, we do not—but it is not that. Could I have warned him?" the young man said, half to himself.

"Warned him of what?"

"His granddaughter Lucy is my friend, you see."

"Course she is—and a nice girl too. What's the matter, Onil?"

The young man shook his head and asked after Michael.

"Still hasn't found that dog of his. You'd better go in and see him."

When the tea and biscuits were finished, Onil knocked at the door and was let in by narrow-nosed, bead-eyed Mrs. King, who seemed genuinely pleased to see him. "If you can do anything with that boy of mine—he's so upset about his blessed dog. I've told him and *told* him it was too big for this house anyway."

Michael King was lying on the black wool hearthrug which had been Sam's bed for five years. "He won't speak, he won't eat," she whispered.

"The dog is still not found?"

"No. Michael, here's Onil and Mr. Makins to see you. Come on, get up!" The boy slowly turned round at his friend's name. Onil was shocked at his appearance. He seemed to have lost pounds in weight.

"Sam must be dead, I know he must be. He'd have found his way home by now if he wasn't."

"That's just not true, Michael," Onil said.

"It is true. Mum says so too. And if he's dead, I don't want to live."

Mrs. King pressed her lips together and said, "Don't talk in that wicked way, Michael."

Onil looked troubled. "Do you want me to help him, Mrs. King?"

"Of course!" she snapped. "If you can talk a bit of sense into him."

"Well, then, Michael, your mother is lying to you when she says she does not know where the dog is. She gave him to the vet, who found a home for him on a farm nine miles from here."

"*What?*"

Michael, white-faced, stared at his mother, who cried in anger and guilt, "It's a lie, it's not true! Who told *you*, anyway? Coming in here so smarmy! Anyway, how did you know? No one in the street did, I made sure of that."

"What's the name of the farm?" Michael asked, taking no notice of his mother.

"Pingold's, North Dean."

Michael was out of the door in a flash. Onil and Mr. Makins followed him, leaving Mrs. King protesting uselessly in the empty room. "I couldn't help it. The dog cost too much to feed—"

"Was that a kind thing to do?" said Harry. "The boy will never trust his mother again. All the same," he added, "what a filthy mean trick to play on the kid. How did you find out?"

"Oh." Onil passed a hand wearily over his eyes. "I can hear people's thoughts."

"*Can* you now?" Harry Makins put his feet reflectively back into the permanganate. "So you know all that goes on inside me, eh?"

"Everything."

"Gawd. That takes some thinking about, dunnit? Do you know," pursued Harry with a fearful curiosity, "do you know when I'm going to die?"

Onil looked at him with tortured eyes. At that moment Lil, haggard and dishevelled, hurried into the court, dropped into the chair beside her husband, and burst into a flood of tears.

"Oh, that poor old man! Oh, what an awful thing! It's shook me all to pieces."

"What, Lil? What has?"

"Poor old Mr. Thatcher. Run over by a motorbike as he was crossing the High Street. Oh, however are we going to tell his poor granddaughter?"

Harry Makins turned his head slowly and stared at Onil. "You said you—you said you could have warned him. Was *that* what you meant?"

"Warned him that it would happen—yes. To prevent it—no."

"Oh, my goodness," Harry said, mostly to himself. "Oh, my goodness. You poor soul. Think of living with a thing like that."

He pulled his feet out of the basin, thrust them dripping into his slippers, and walked heavily indoors.

That evening no one came to visit Onil at the hospital.

"They're afraid," he said sadly to little Nurse Thatcher, who was back on nights—she had said she would prefer to go on working if no one objected. "They're afraid I shall tell them when they are going to die."

"*I'm* not scared," she said, and gently tucked his wing under the sheet.

"They won't come to see me any more."

But he was wrong. Father Fogarty turned up and after some beating about the bush came to the point.

"My boy," he said, "if that's how life is on Mars, I can quite see why you wanted to leave. It must be terrible. I'm used to God having access to my thoughts, but the neighbours too—no. Well, you can see how it is."

"Yes," Onil said sadly. "You won't want me here. And I had hoped I was going to be so useful in the library—"

"You'll find somewhere else, my boy, somewhere just as good, with that grand little spaceship of yours. I've sealed up the crack with Polymix, and if I were you I'd get going just as soon as you feel strong enough. The people in the town are very sorry—they don't bear any hard feelings—but they just don't like the thought of seeing you any more.

"*Au revoir* then, my dear fellow; send a picture postcard to let us know how you are getting on—"

The door shut behind him.

Wordlessly, Nurse Thatcher began moving Onil's one or two little oddments out of his locker.

"Oh, well," he said. "It's a fine moonlit night for a flight. And that did look quite a nice little planet, the one with the five green moons—"

"And the partridge in the pear tree."

"If only it weren't so uninhabited."

"I'm coming too," said Nurse Thatcher.

"Lucy! You mustn't think of such a thing."

"You can't stop me! *I* don't mind," said Lucy firmly. "*I* don't mind your knowing what I'm thinking." And she gave him such a clear and beautiful look as she stood in the moonlight pressing six handkerchiefs and a cake of soap against her white starched bib that that was the end of the matter.

An hour later, as he bicycled dreamily homeward from North Dean with Sam loping beside him, Michael King saw the white ship burst upwards like a giant Ping-pong ball from its nest in Viners' Court.

At first he grieved for the loss of his friend.

"But never mind, Sam," he said consolingly, "in eight years I'll be old enough to be a space pilot, and then we'll go up to Sirun and see the five green moons and the four blue seas and the three extinct volcanoes. . . ."

And two turtle doves and a partridge in a pear tree.

Sultan's Splash

"NORMAN is free now, Henry," the secretary said, and gave him a five-amp smile. Through Norman's open door—Dobbs-Journeyman Publicity discouraged closed office doors and was known to ease out executives who were overkeen on privacy—the copy chief had been visible reading *The New Yorker* for the last five minutes, but Henry pretended not to have noticed this. As he entered, Norman began to scuffle in an important way among the papers on his desk. Henry patiently studied the familiar props: the fever-pink carpet, the palm tree growing upside down from the ceiling with the Dobbs-Journeyman slogan, "We can lick Gravity too," wreathed about its trunk. It needed pruning.

Norman looked up with a dazzling smile.

"Well, Henry! What can we do for you so early in the morning?"

"I'd like the day off, Norman, if you don't mind. My aunt's dying."

The smile grew infinitesimally less dazzling.

"Rather a *banal* excuse, dear boy?"

Someone had once said in Norman's hearing that if he had gone into the church he would have made a good cardinal, and since then he had adopted a subtly paternal attitude towards his staff, giving them inscrutable Monsignor-like smiles and encouraging them to confide in him by a manner that combined teasing camaraderie with honest, manly sympathy. On some people it worked very well. He slumped back in his swivel chair now and regarded Henry quizzically; he was a squarely built man with a square smiling face, a mass of curly black hair, and an unusually large mouth. His copywriters said that you could see Norman smiling even when you stood behind his back. He wore a white suit and a rosebud in his buttonhole.

"You know, Henry boy, if you take many more days off, I shall begin to think you don't *love* us? And since you *have* dropped in, I think I should mention that your work lately has been just a scrap—shall we say—uninspired? Maybe we don't stimulate you enough here, Henry? I wonder if another job, just for a breath of fresh air, might be beneficial? Just for a couple of years, say? Then, *of course*, we'd welcome you back with open arms."

Of course, Henry thought, if I came with a lot of other people's ideas.

"I'm sure Blather and Pother would *jump* at the chance of securing you," Norman ended, beaming, his eyes Cheshire-cat slits of fun and friendship. With a strong effort, Henry refrained from putting his hand into the pocket where Blather and Pother's letter regretted they could not avail themselves of his talent at present.

"But to return to your story, dear child. Ah, if only some of this imagination could be canalised!"

"I'm afraid it's the truth," Henry said stolidly, and held out a telegram. It read: I SHALL DIE TONIGHT AT 10.08 P.M. CAN YOU ARRANGE TO BE THERE. LURLINE HAMMERSTALL.

Norman raised his brows over this. "Suicide?" he inquired.

"No, she's always said she'd have a presentiment when the time came. She's ninety-five."

"Lurline Hammerstall," mused Norman. "Why does that name ring a bell?"

"She was a romantic novelist in the nineties. *A Broken Blossom, Ten Days in the Desert, Passion's Oasis.*"

"Of course. And didn't she run off to Constantinople with the Chancellor of the Exchequer?"

"Baghdad with the Foreign Secretary," Henry corrected. "Lord Barbilliard. It was a famous scandal."

"So it was. People sang a song about it, didn't they:

I'd rather ride on a camel with Barbie
Than frivol at Ascot or win on the Derby;
I'd rather spoon by the Sphinx with Lurline
Than speak to the Commons or chat with the Queen.

What ever became of Barbilliard?"

"He died in the desert in some obscure way; I think it was said he caught a tropical disease. Lurline subsequently married the Sheikh Ibn al Fuaz el Mezzat al Kebir. When *he* died, twenty years later, she came back to England with her three-legged crocodile and settled down in Dorset. I'm her great-nephew and only living relative."

"What glamour, my dear! Of course I can see that you must certainly be at her deathbed. Perhaps she'll leave you a fortune—her books sold like hot cakes in the nineties, didn't they?"

"She spent all the money on *confort moderne* for the Sheikh; she has nothing but an annuity."

"Too bad," Norman said gaily. "Well—think over our chat on your trip, won't you? By the way, I'm moving you off your present accounts—just for a little change, just for a breath of fresh air."

"What are you giving me?" Henry asked, with a horrible sinking feeling.

"Speedwell Butter."

"Nothing else?"

"Just to concentrate your abilities, dear child. So be thinking up some *really* scintillating, really creative ideas for tomorrow, will you, and we'll have a little meeting as soon as you come in."

Speedwell Butter! If Norman had thrown a lump of the stuff at him, the news could not have come with a more dismal squelch. Speedwell Butter, made, allegedly, from residues of several other butters and cooking fats, had been a nonseller for twenty years, and was among the dregs at the bottom of the Dobbs-Journeyman barrel. Sitting in the train, Henry let his mind teeter distractedly between apprehensions of his aunt's deathbed—what did one do at a deathbed, anyway?—and alarm at the poverty-stricken quality of his ideas about butter. The only thing in Speedwell's favour was that it cost little more than other brands:

it had an unpleasant oily taste and tended to disintegrate to a puddle if the thermometer rose more than a few degrees above zero centigrade. Henry saw dismissal staring him in the face; he would not be the first copywriter sped out of Dobbs-Journeyman on a Speedwell slide.

An aged taxi met him at Loose Chippings station; the driver gave the impression of having only just removed a straw from his mouth.

"So the old lady's failing at last?" he said as they ground along the high-banked lanes. "Ah, she'll be a sad loss, she will. They don't come like that no more. She'll be missed despert bad in these parts, that's suttin."

"Oh?" Henry said. "I'd no idea she was a well-known character."

"She be mortial clever wi' her unguments and linimations; ah, her linctuary for Megrim of the Bowel have saved many a soul from old Dr. Wassop's clutches. Folk comes to her from far and near for poltuses and elixatives."

If this was so, it was plain that Miss Hammerstall made no great profit from her activities, for her cottage was dilapidated to a degree and could hardly be seen for the unpruned creepers smothering its exterior. The front garden was overgrown and neglected, but rows of neat plants were visible at the rear, casting long shadows in the light of the setting sun. Miss Hammerstall herself stood by the gate, bidding affectionate good-bye to a pretty dark-haired girl who looked rather tearful and carried a basket.

"Ah, Henry! How good of you to come. Tansy, this is my nephew, Henry Hammerstall; my goddaughter, Tansy Argew. Adieu, then, Tansy, precious girl; I know you will remember all I've told you. Henry, come in; you must be dying for food."

Aunt Lurline did not look as if she were within four hours of presumptive death, nor did she look ninety-five; she might have been a healthy, wind-browned sixty. Traces of great beauty remained in her delicate, aquiline features, and her eyes were remarkable: a dark, Mediterranean blue, unfaded by age.

Over couscous, kebabs, and Turkish coffee, she explained why she had asked Henry to come.

"You hear that knocking, dear boy?"

Not being deaf, he could hardly fail to. He had been thinking it an odd time to inaugurate what sounded like extensive repairs to the roof.

"No, it isn't workmen, it's rappings. Spirits, that is to say. I sent you the telegram as soon as it started; Barbie always promised he'd give me twenty-four hours' warning. Dear me, I *am* looking forward to seeing Barbie again; he was always so entertaining, dear fellow! That's why I asked you down, Henry. I fear I am sadly out of touch with public affairs now, and I know Barbie will expect to hear all the latest political gossip, so I want you to spend the next few hours giving me a good briefing. Oh, before you start I should mention that I have made you my literary executor."

Henry expressed his gratification.

"There's no money in it," Lurline said frankly. "All my books have long been out of print—unless you can do something with my unpublished manuscript—*Jottings from a Desert Diary.*" She gave him a large battered black folder crammed with loose and rather grimy pages. "Tansy, of course, inherits the cottage, which would be of no use to you; she will keep on my practice and look after the herbs and the crocodile pool."

"Pool?"

"In memory of poor Fuaz, you remember him? He died three years ago, faithful fellow; crocodiles do not really thrive in this climate. There's his anklet hanging on the wall."

Henry remembered that the crocodile had always worn a gold band on his right foreleg.

"But now, Henry, to work! From dear Barbie's rappings I infer he is just as impatient as I for our reunion, so pray, without delay, tell me all the scandals; you are such a young man of affairs! Which party is in power at present, and who is premier?"

The next three hours were almost as exacting for Henry as one of Norman's little meetings, but he came through with fair credit; luckliy he took a keen interest in current affairs (he would have liked to go in for politics had he not been under the sad necessity of earning a living) and was friendly with several Fleet Street journalists, so that he was able to give Lurline the the inside stories she demanded.

At a few minutes past ten she said, "Thank you, my dear boy;

you have been a great help. Now, I had better just powder my nose—*so*—and a touch of perfume—Fuaz was always so fond of this Attar of Roses." Henry wondered if she was referring to the crocodile or to her second husband, the Sheikh Ibn al Fuaz.

"By the way," she said, "if there is anything you don't understand among the jottings, Tansy will help you. But remember—discretion always! There are some powerful . . ."

Her voice died away. Henry looked at his watch. It was exactly 10.08 p.m. The rappings had ceased and the cottage was extremely quiet. He gently and respectfully covered his aunt's face with a fold of her lace burnous, went up to bed, and slept soundly.

Next day, having left the funeral arrangements in the capable hands of Tansy and Dr. Wassop, he caught a train back to London and spent the journey absorbed in Lurline's *Desert Jottings.*

> JUNE 7TH, 1889. By caravan across Rub' al Khali; at Little Hufhuf Oasis we encountered Sheikh Ibn al Fuaz el Mezzat al Kebir with his retinue. The sheikh v. gracious. Invited us both to sherbet.
>
> JUNE 9TH. Sheikh I. al F. el M. al K. suggested we continue our journey together. I was delighted at prospect, but Barbie less so; he has not altogether taken to Fuaz; says some of his ideas not cricket!! I, however, find the Sheikh a *complete gentleman.* Unfortunately desert life does not really suit Barbie; the insects annoy him terribly & he misses his club.
>
> JUNE 18TH. Sheikh Fuaz lent me Arab mare, took me on delightful gallop after antelope. Scenery v. romantic!!! A most exhilarating excursion. Barbie, I am sorry to say, remained in tent all day, *sulking.* In evening played chess with S.F.
>
> JULY 4TH. Fuaz has given me a collar of pink pearls in requital for rubbing his housemaid's knee. Such a pretty colour! B. v. disagreeable; says in any case they will *fade.* Chess again in evening; French defence.

Here, unfortunately, there came a gap in the journal; all these entries had been written on one sheet, and, search as he would,

Henry could not find the continuation. The next sheet began in the middle.

> . . . still miss poor B. sadly. Who would have expected such a result from the immersion?! But perhaps it was for the best. Desert life did *not* suit him & he had repeatedly begged me to return with him to Weybridge. He is happier as it is. Sh. Fuaz *most* gentlemanly & considerate; begs me to look on the Royal Tent as my own, & has presented me with a *delicious* opal-studded belt. Also provided a portable water tank, thoughtful creature! Chess till 2 a.m.

What could be the use of the portable water tank? Henry wondered. The journal did not declare. He browsed on, finding a thread of narrative here and a thread there, casually mixed among oriental-sounding recipes, purple patches of verse, some unskilled but evocative sketches of camels, robed figures, and palm-trees, remedies for illnesses, historical and topographical notes. In fact a sort of Arabian Mrs. Beeton, he mused, reading on.

> The Camel. A useful but ill-condition'd animal which, on account of its curious Stomach, can travel for ??? miles without water at ??? miles per hour. To cure camel-gall: immerse the afflicted part in Hot Tar for half an hour. (Considerable force and resolution are needed.)

From this time on, it was plain, progress towards matrimony between Lurline and the Sheikh was swift and unimpeded.

> AUGUST 9TH. Today I and my dear, *dear* Fuaz became Man & Wife. Oh, how happy it makes me to write these words!!! He has given me a wonderful set of chessmen—rubies and black diamonds—& ordered new carpets for Tent.
>
> SEPTEMBER 20TH. Have been attempting to interest Fuaz in *English cookery*; he is laughably suspicious of such things as our good oatmeal porridge, boiled cod, etc. Tried to convince him that a diet of food cooked largely in rancid oil not *altogether beneficial.*

A number of recipes followed.

Henry was now mystified by several references to Barbie. Could Barbilliard, after all, be still alive, playing some melancholy gooseberry role? But it soon became clear that the Barbie referred to was, in fact, a pet crocodile belonging to Lurline, the first, presumably, of the dynasty ending with three-legged Fuaz.

SEPTEMBER 30TH. Fuaz has given me a silver chain for dear Barbie. He looks so sweet in it, the links flashing as we toss him fish!

OCTOBER 2ND. Eureka! I have at last found a way to make porridge palatable to Fuaz. Who would have thought it possible to make porridge crisp and crunchy! But it can be done!! And so simply!!! Old Fatima, the great-aunt by marriage, is indeed a treasure house of lore. I believe this process could also be used on oil & might prevent it turning rancid. Must experiment. . . .

Several years, it seemed, then elapsed happily and uneventfully, spent in roaming about the desert from one set of in-laws to another. Only one mishap marred the idyll.

AUGUST 9TH. Horrible catastrophe!! Fuaz had his left hand bitten off by B., whom he was teasing with a piece of fish. I felt oblig'd to point out that if he had not acquired this unkind habit the accident wd not have occur'd. Have dressed the Limb with Hot Tar & Fuaz is well enough but much agitated & has ordered B to be destroyed. I, too, greatly afflicted, indeed a seething ferment of vain regrets. But it is true B hd become rather Large and Dangerous. I shall lose no opportunity of procuring a successor.

Thinking the matter over, in the light of what F. told me before she died, the accident seems little more than *Poetic Justice.*

"To clarify camel fat . . .

Henry looked up and found his train entering the terminus. Hastily he bundled Lurline's manuscript into his briefcase and dived for a taxi, his mind awhirl with crocodiles, camels, and minarets. What had F. told Lurline before she died? And why was it poetic justice to have your left hand bitten off by a crocodile?

The taxi pulled up outside Dobbs-Journeyman's offices in High Holborn. Henry paid and took the lift up to his office. It was not until he saw the *Urgent* note, signed Norman Garple, that he remembered his last interview. Good heavens, Speedwell Butter! He had not given it a thought for the last twelve hours.

"*Here's* our wandering boy," Norman said with his indulgent smile. "And I've no doubt he's teeming with creative ideas after his little jaunt. I'll just introduce you round the Speedwell group, Henry, and then we're all agog to know what you've thought up for us."

Henry heard no word of the introductions. His mind was, as Lurline would have said, a seething ferment of vain regrets. But there was no use crying over spilt butter. The best thing would be to wait till Norman had finished speaking and then tender a dignified resignation; perhaps he could let it be inferred that Lurline had, after all, left him an unexpected legacy.

"I leave Speedwell Butter in Henry's capable hands," Norman said, and sat on a corner of a table looking receptive and anticipatory.

Henry stood up to speak.

"We all know what's the matter with Speedwell Butter," he was surprised to find himself saying. "The price is okay, but it has a nasty taste and an oily consistency. I suggest that we ignore the taste for the time, but get the client to produce the butter in a crystallised form, and launch an all-out campaign on the theme '*Crisp, Crunchy Speedwell Butter Puts the Crunch in Lunch.*' "

He paused and looked to see what effect his words were having. The group was gazing at him bug-eyed, open-mouthed, uncertain whether to laugh.

"Dear boy," Norman said silkily. "Such a sense of *fun.*"

"I'm serious," Henry said. "I have notes of a process here that is guaranteed to crystallise any food with a sloppy, oily consistency. Like butter. Or porridge. Would you like to see it demonstrated?"

He pulled Lurline's recipe out of his briefcase, praying that it would work as well in the cold English climate as under the hot skies of Arabia.

"You really mean this?" Norman said. "We don't have to ring for a psychiatrist?"

"Sure I mean it. Have we any butter?"

"Rilla," said Norman to his secretary, "bring butter. And porridge. What else will you need?" he asked Henry.

"Tartar—sodium silicate—starch—ice—one or two other things. I'll go over and get them from the home economics department."

"I'll ring them, dear child—just tell me what you want." Norman made rapid notes.

An amazing feeling of power and exhilaration took command of Henry. Even Norman now seemed impressed by his confidence. When a girl from the kitchens brought the required ingredients and a portable hotplate, he handled them with the certainty of a conjuror.

"Which shall we begin with—butter? I clarify it in a saucepan, add this—this—and this, stir briskly, chill rapidly and—there you have it. Simple, isn't it? Crisp, crunchy butter."

He shook the saucepan. Sure enough, it was filled with opaque yellow crystals the size of corn kernels.

"Equally delicious on toast, bread, or crackers," he said, shovelling the crystals on to a sheet of blotting paper. "Doesn't affect the flavour at all. It's exactly the same process for porridge, only of course you get grey crystals. Crisp, crunchy porridge . . ."

"Boy," whispered Tom Tocksin, the TV director, "you've revolutionised the food industry. Just wait till the client hears of this."

"I think I'd better get on the line to them," Norman said, looking preoccupied. "They'll be delighted, I'm sure. It's great stuff, Henry, great! I suggest we all adjourn till after lunch, half-past two, everybody? Right."

Henry floated back to his room on unaccustomed waves of triumph. Most of the Speedwell group came with him, and it was natural that they should all float together down to The Fighting Cocks to celebrate Henry's stroke of genius. But after half an hour Tom Tocksin suddenly slamed his glass on the counter and exclaimed,

"Fools that we are! You ought to be down at the patent office. Get a taxi, quick!"

"Patent office?"

"Staking your claim, oaf! Hurry!"

Too late! By the time Henry had found his way to the right department, Patent OOXZA/79658532Q, *Method of Crystallising Liquescent Foodstuffs,* was already pending, registered under the name of Norman Garple.

Three weeks later Norman left Dobbs-Journeyman to become a director of Speedwell Crunchy Fools Ltd.; in six months he was a millionaire.

Henry was pardonably annoyed at this turn of events. True, he had been given a small increase in salary, but by and large he felt that things had turned out inequitably. The thought of Lurline irritated him so much that he thrust her manuscript into a bottom drawer until a publisher, learning that the world-shaking invention of crunchy butter stemmed from one of her desert recipes, rang up and asked to see *Jottings from a Desert Diary.*

"I'd better put the pages in order and get it typed out first," Henry said. "It's in a frightful mess." With belated caution he had remembered that there might be other epoch-making household hints in the journal.

He began laboriously typing it out, but was soon in difficulties with Lurline's handwriting, particularly over measurements and ingredients in the recipes. At this point he recalled Tansy, Lurline's goddaughter. Perhaps she could help? He sent her a card, inviting himself for a weekend to the pub at Loose Chippings.

Six weeks later Henry rang up Norman Garple and asked if they could meet. Norman was his usual urbane self, but difficult to pin down.

"I'm so busy, dear boy—there's hardly time to breathe. But perhaps I could fit you in just for a few minutes—at my office, say round about six on Thursday evening? That suit?"

"Excellent," Henry agreed cordially.

The Speedwell offices were emptying fast when Henry arrived for his appointment. A secretary let him in, put on her hat, and hurried down the stairs. Norman, looking high level and harassed, nodded to him in a bitten-off fashion.

"The commercial hurly-burly, Henry—it's hideous, really hideous. I can't tell you how I long for the dear old creative days at Dobbs-J. Well, what can I do for you, boy? Anything to help a friend from auld lang syne."

"I've come to you for advice, really," Henry said with a diffident air. "Of course it's cheek, but you have such a lot of know-how when it comes to marketing. I thought perhaps you'd have some suggestions about a new product."

"Which new product is that?" Norman asked alertly.

"It's something else from old Lurline's journal. Really that turns out to be very good value. This new thing is one of her Arabian notions, picked up from an old great-aunt of Ibn al Fuaz. You know the Arabs are great on fancy baths—when they get hold of some water, that is; well, this is a sort of bath-foam powder, invented long before the days of detergents. Fuaz used to have it made up specially; I thought maybe it could be sold as a bath essence for men, called something Arabian Nightish like Sultan's Splash."

"Sounds a possibility," said Norman. "What's it like?"

"Not bad at all," Henry told him with carefully moderate enthusiasm. "You put a spoonful in your bath and it really does make you feel a different person. After five minutes soaking you're relaxed and vigorous and wide awake. Like to try it?"

"Love to, dear boy. You've brought some with you? Good show. I'm going straight on to a cocktail party, matter of fact, so I'll just pop a spoonful in the directors' tub. . . ."

The police were not inclined to connect the disappearance of Mr. Norman Garple with the coincidental discovery of a medium-sized crocodile in the directors' bath at the Speedwell offices. They did, however, arrest Henry, as the last person known to have seen Garple alive, and he had a difficult time convincing a sceptical chief superintendent that he had performed an Arabian Nights trick on his ex-business associate.

"Look, I can only prove that my story is true by doing it again, can't I?" he said reasonably. "And who's going to volunteer to be the guinea pig? No, I can't undo the effects, and so far as Garple's concerned I don't want to. There's no law against turning a man into a crocodile."

In the end, as the police remained tiresomely intransigent, Henry's lawyers advertised for someone genuinely fed up with life. The thousands of replies were gradually sifted down to one candidate: Albert Weeks, a sad, defeated little ex–swimming instructor whose wife would not let him go in the water in case he had heart failure. Life had been robbed of meaning for him. When he understood the case he gladly immersed himself in a bathful of Sultan's Splash and became an undoubted crocodile. This convinced the police, Henry was released, and the two crocodiles were given to the zoo (where they received kind treatment and lived long, socially useful lives).

"I suppose Fuaz the crocodile really was Ibn al Fuaz," Henry observed to Tansy some days later as they strolled hand in hand through the garden at Loose Chippings. "Lurline must have been annoyed when she discovered the trick he'd played on Barbie, and turned the tables."

"I think Barbilliard was always her real love," Tansy said. "She began to suspect that Fuaz had used a love potion. Oh, excuse me, talking of love potions, I promised to take one along to Dr. Wassup's receptionist. I shan't be gone long."

Henry and Tansy were married the next year. This would have delighted Lurline, who had, indeed, planned it. They lived comfortably; moreover, Lurline's practice and film rights from the *Desert Jottings* provided a steady income and, although Sultan's Splash never went into regular commercial production, Henry achieved his ambition to enter politics by making small quantities of it discreetly available to his own party for the removal of undesirable parliamentary opponents. The number of crocodiles in the zoo increased materially in the next few years.

Henry's devotion to his wife was undoubted, whether or not it had been boosted by any recourse to love potions on Tansy's part, but, until the end of his life he had a curious phobia about baths, preferring to take them when his wife was out of the house, and always carefully rinsing the bath first with a strong solution of carbolic before venturing to set foot in it.

The Far Forests

THEY were playing Twenty Questions in the study of the old vicarage. The room was full of the gentle ticktock of clocks—one on the desk, one on the mantelpiece, not to mention the grandfather in the hall adding his slow, thoughtful reminder that, even in this retreat, time moved on its measured way.

Outside, the night wind stirred the branches of ancient trees.

"Is it plankton?" said Miss Dallas, concealing a yawn. For years past, Twenty Questions had bored her to tears, but her brother, the old Canon, had a childish delight in the game, and so she indulged him.

"My dear Delia!" he said mildly. "Plankton would be animal, not vegetable. Have another question. That leaves you with three to go."

"Seaweed, then. If it's vegetable and not on any continent or island, it *must* be in the sea."

The parchment-like wrinkles round his eyes extended at this evidence of her feminine illogicality.

"Think, Delia! There are other elements."

Miss Dallas looked round the room for inspiration. The ginger-brown velvet curtains were drawn, the fire slumbered in its black marble grate. A Persian cat, almost as elderly as the brother and sister, slept on the worn bearskin hearthrug. Innumerable books held dust and memories. A clutter of objects on the mantelpiece, never to be thrown away, included fronds of dried-up palm from the Holy Land, a paperweight from Florence, some curious lumps of rock from the Aegean, an ammonite, porcupine quills, and a silver statue of a seraph with three pairs of wings.

"Well, I've never heard of vegetables floating in the air," Miss Dallas said impatiently. "Is it thistledown?"

"No. One more."

"I give up."

"Think!"

But she refused to think any more, finding thought a troublesome exercise. She got up and began tidying the room with a sort of affectionate exasperation. The Canon eyed her mildly. He resembled the White Knight—his eyes were set deeply in great hollows, his large, noble, polished brow sloped back into a sparse halo of white thistledown, he had a smile of great sweetness and a general air of being slightly mad.

"No," said Miss Dallas decisively. "I give up. What was it?"

"The forests of Mars."

"*Mars?*"

"Don't you remember that TV programme the other night? The scientist who said the red patches might be forests?"

"It's not proved," Miss Dallas snapped. "You should have called it abstract, not vegetable. You can't count that as a point."

"Very well, my dear," he said patiently. "That makes me three thousand, three hundred, and ninety-four and you two thousand, nine hundred, and seventeen. You are catching me up. Now I shall just go out for a stroll while you brew the cocoa."

"Don't be long," she said, turning out the oil lamp. "It's a very dark night."

The Canon was occasionally known to lose his memory and wander away. Sometimes he was found and returned by a devoted parishioner; sometimes he returned of his own accord after intervals of varying length, amounting once to five days. He never knew where he had been. His sister worried about it a little, but not unduly, relying, perhaps with reason, on his appearance of obvious saintliness to protect him from harm. But she did try to guard him from catching a chill.

"Henry! Your goloshes."

"Oh, yes. Yes, my dear. You do not happen to know, do you, where they are? I seem to have mislaid them."

Miss Dallas lit a candle and searched impatiently among the clutter of umbrellas, walking sticks, gumboots, shooting sticks, Victorian-looking lawn-tennis racquets, polo clubs (what were *they* still doing here?) in the front hall. The goloshes were presently found in the laundry basket.

"I cannot think how they got there," said the Canon resignedly, and ambled out through the trellised porch into the garden.

It was indeed a dark night. Not a single star could be seen; the sky seemed as low as the vicarage roof. Not a sound came from the village, three-quarters of a mile distant. The Canon thought contentedly, as he strolled on the velvety lawn under his walnut trees (although the night was black, he knew to a hairsbreadth where each tree stood), that his house in its acre of garden might as well have been isolated in a thousand miles of woodland, even on a planet of its own. It was so dark, and the air smelt of leaves.

Delia called and he returned dutifully, sighing, to the kitchen door.

"Leave your goloshes by the stove, then you'll know where to look in the morning."

"So I shall, my dear, so I shall."

"And drink your cocoa while it's hot."

Notwithstanding this reminder the Canon went off several times into a dream as he sipped. "You know, my dear," he emerged once to say, "in spite of your scepticism I like to think there are forests on Mars. In these sad days of deforestation—do you remember that distressing programme we watched on land erosion in Kenya?—it gives me pleasure to think that at least on another planet there may be huge tracts of virgin forest, quite unspoilt by human cupidity. How many trees did the man say had to be cut down each day to produce one issue of *The New York Times*?"

"I can't remember," said Miss Dallas shortly. "But has it occurred to you, Henry, that if there are forests on Mars there may also be inhabitants, cutting them down?"

"Oh, no," said the Canon, gently but firmly. "I am sure that if there are beings on Mars they are of a high enough order of intelligence and integrity to leave the forests unspoiled."

"Well—" said Miss Dallas, softening, "I hope you are right." For she, like her brother, remembered with great happiness their childhood in the Forest of Dean. "Good night, Henry. Straight to bed now. No wandering about." She gave his cheek a brisk peck.

"No, indeed," said the Canon, turning absently towards the back door. She redirected him to bed. As she rinsed the cups and saucepan she heard him upstairs, singing his evening hymn:

"That, when black darkness closes day,
And shadows thicken round our way,
Faith may no darkness know, and night
From faith's clear beam may borrow light. . . ."

Like all the old, the Canon slept lightly and woke early. Next morning he was up at half-past five, and after paying a visit to his cherished lepidoptera collection in the spare room, he went in search of his goloshes, intending to take an early-morning stroll, as he often did before his sister came down.

The downstairs part of the house, with curtains drawn, was still veiled in twilight. It was a close, dark, quiet morning. The leaves, as so often on a grey morning in early summer, seemed to take all light from the sky. No birds were singing.

"I fear it will rain later," said the Canon, unlocking the back door, and forgetting his goloshes. He stepped out, and paused in mild surprise. For the green, hushed darkness was quite as intense outside the house as inside—in fact, the whole sky was obscured by a dull and glaucous pall which lay close above the tops of the vicarage trees.

"What a remarkable phenomenon," said the Canon. "Can it presage a typhoon or hurricane? I can remember observing this curious opacity and greenness of sky in the tropics, before such storms. But the atmosphere is not electric, nor unduly warm. The light is certainly most strange. Shall I awaken Delia? But no, poor girl, she has such a busy life. I will let her sleep a little longer."

He strolled away from the house, enjoying the pleasant gloom.

"And what a powerful—what an *unusually* powerful smell of vegetation," he said. "I suppose it is the moisture in the air drawing out scents from the leaves, but really, even for this time of year, I do not recall ever having experienced anything quite like it. The odour is aromatic—like that of walnut leaves—but yet there is something stronger and quite distinctive. . . ."

He paused, and his voice trailed away.

He was now standing at the extremity of his garden, beyond a little orchard of apple and pear trees which ran from the far end of the lawn to a brook. The babbling of the water was very loud in the quietness. The dark green sky seemed even lower here—seemed to be resting like a tent on the tips of the pear branches, some of which were still hung with blossoms. As he watched it, this tentlike sky appeared to bulge and sway.

"One would almost believe," the Canon murmured, "that some bird had alighted—but it must be the effect of the approaching storm. Dear me—and I have forgotten my goloshes."

But next moment he had forgotten them again, for the improbable happened, and a rent appeared in the green membrane of sky. A clear, three-cornered patch of brightness showed beyond it and rapidly extended, flooding daylight on to the blossoming branches and bluebell-starred grass below. The startled birds immediately began to sing.

"Can it be," said Canon Dallas, "that something is *nibbling* the sky?"

He continued to watch attentively and was confirmed in his opinion. Other rents appeared, and the greenness curled back rapidly, like fronds of burning paper. More and more daylight poured into the orchard, and soon the Canon was able to see the creatures that were demolishing this dark canopy.

There was not a doubt about it, they were moths. But of a size! Four of them, each rather larger than a tractor, were hovering twenty feet up, rapidly munching and consuming the green coverlet that lay over the vicarage and its surrounding land. A shred of green the size of a tablecloth fluttered down beside the Canon, and a long proboscis followed it down and caught it as it fell.

The Canon stood rapt, gazing up. He was not in the least alarmed. True, not all moths were vegetarian, but these ones appeared to be so, for if they were moths, and they must be, what could they be eating but a single gigantic leaf that had fallen from heaven knew where, completely covering the vicarage?

At first he was too absorbed in the beauty of the moths to think of anything else. Their hovering wings moved too fast for a clear view—all that he saw was a shimmering blur of iridescent purple and black and green—but their bodies, covered with thick, soft golden fur, could plainly be seen, as well as their long antennae and great lambent eyes. They had almost finished the leaf now—only a few shreds remained.

One of the moths settled on the lawn for a moment or two and put itself to rights, businesslike as a cat, shaking its fur into place, folding and unfolding its wings. The Canon gave an incredulous gasp at the sudden spread of colour, damasked in unimagined shades of unimagined brilliance.

"Oh!" he cried. "Wait! Don't go—please don't go!"

But it was too late. The moths, communicating silently by means of their antennae, had risen and were fluttering together, seeking, it seemed, the right direction.

"Just a moment longer—oh, please!"

Did they turn their great shining eyes on him in pity? They hovered an instant, and then as if carried by a thermal current soared together up and up, past the pale early-morning sun, until his dazzled eyes could follow them no farther.

He turned, stricken, to search the orchard for some relic of their presence, a frond of golden fur, scrap of leaf, anything—but it almost seemed as if they had been bent on removing all evidence of themselves: there was nothing. Nothing at all.

"Their fur was golden," the Canon said, spooning down his porridge. "And their wings were—oh, every colour, and as wide across as a cricket pitch. Their eyes were—" What colour had their eyes been? A steely blue? Gold? Crystalline? He found it hard to remember. "I shall write to *The Times*," he said. "And ask in the village. Find out if anyone else saw them. Oh, Delia, I am sorry I had no time to wake you. They were gone so quickly."

He was silent again, numb with the anguish of their departure without him. Oh, to have gone with those travellers, to have shared their voyage and seen the forests that nurtured them!

His sister was looking at him with troubled eyes.

"You're sure you're all right, Henry? You haven't caught a chill, going out like that without your goloshes?"

"Of course not, Delia," he said somewhat impatiently. "If it matters to you so much, I will put my goloshes on now, before I write my letter to *The Times*."

Nobody in the village had seen the moths, and *The Times* was too cautious to publish, without additional confirmation, such a communication from an eighty-five-year-old Canon who was well known to be somewhat dreamy and prone to fits of absent-mindedness; his letter was put aside to wait for others. People were kind to the Canon about his vision, for everybody was fond of him; but it did gradually become apparent to him that nobody really believed he had seen the moths—or not with his physical eyes at any rate. His feelings were hurt, and he stopped talking about the incident, even to Delia. But deep in his heart he cherished the faint, faint hope that some day the moths would come back.

Time passed, summer waned, autumn came. Miss Dallas went off one day on a Women's Institute outing, and the Canon made haste to seize such a golden opportunity for cutting down the brambles at the end of the orchard, a job he greatly enjoyed. The sight of her brother with a billhook in his hand always filled Miss Dallas with terror, and if she had known his intentions she would have circumvented him by getting a man up from the village.

After working for half an hour he laid bare a large object which had been buried in nettles and brambles and half sunk in the grass. It seemed to be spherical, about as large as a piano, not hard, sticky, faintly iridescent.

He laid down the billhook and began clearing away the brambles with trembling hands, wonder and hope and incredulous joy growing in his heart. The hope was justified. Unmistakably, what lay among the cut vegetation was a crumpled corner of the great leaf, sere and brown now, but still slightly aromatic, wrapped about a gigantic cocoon.

His first thought was, "I shall see one of them again! I have another chance." His second thought was, "People will believe me now." His first worry was, "What shall I feed it on when it comes out?"

He fetched the wheelbarrow and transported the cocoon with immense care (it was not heavy) to the disused vicarage stables. He decided, for the moment at least, to say nothing of his discovery to anyone, not even to Delia. Delia would fuss, and take his temperature, and make him put on his goloshes; and for the rest, there would be commotion and publicity and undesirable visitors—they might even take the cocoon away and put it in the Natural History Museum, or decide it belonged to the Crown. And he did want, he wanted so terribly badly, to see the unbelievable colours on those wings once more, in peace and solitude. Was it selfish of him? he wondered, or was it, perhaps, what the moths would have wished?

So he kept silent through the winter, remembered his goloshes, remembered to drink his cocoa when it was hot, chatted to his parishioners, and preached a sermon in the cathedral from time to time. And if he seemed more than usually vague and preoccupied—if the sermons were more than usually dreamy and full of unexplained allusions—well, as people said to one another, after all, the old Canon's getting on and he's really wonderful for his age.

Only to his sister did he sometimes still talk about the forests of Mars.

"The tragedy of it is," he said, "that we may have spoiled our chances of seeing them. They must know that we have wrecked our own forests—naturally they won't, if they can help it, give us the opportunity of doing the same to theirs. If they can help it, they won't even let us know those forests exist."

"Who won't let us?"

"The inhabitants," he said, and his eyes became filled with inner visions of wonderful colours. "But perhaps they'd let just one or two go, people of proved integrity; but why should I be so foolish as to think that?" And he looked so humble and dejected that Miss Dallas, worried, insisted on his taking a dose.

The Canon presently took steps unknown to his sister. He bought two enormous drums of honey and put them in the disused stable beside the cocoon. Winter slowly passed and May came round again.

"Do you think it's good for you to spend so much time in the old stables?" Miss Dallas said. "You are becoming quite thin and pale. I think I must get you away for a holiday, to Broadstairs or Bournemouth."

"On no account—I mean, not just yet," her brother said hurriedly. "I feel extremely well, Delia."

Next week Miss Dallas was obliged to go to London for an annual conference of Women's Organisations. She left her brother anxiously. He had hardly seen her off before he hastened back to the stable where the cocoon was beginning to move and make faint noises. He fetched a chair and sat patiently, hour after hour, forgetting to eat or sleep in his intense excitement.

Only once did he leave the stables, and then it was to fetch a hammer and chisel to break open the drums of honey.

When Miss Dallas returned from her conference, the Canon was nowhere to be found. At first she was not seriously alarmed, for the weather was warm and dry, but when a day had gone by, and then three days, and then three weeks, and still the police had found no trace of him, she became desperate.

Country-wide appeals were broadcast, prayers were said in the parish church and in the cathedral, but still no one came forward to say that an elderly white-haired clergyman with a mild and benevolent expression had been found wandering.

And then one night when Miss Dallas, grimly blinking back her tears, was just about to heat the milk for a solitary cup of cocoa, the kitchen door opened and her brother walked in. Just like that! Mild, serene, unruffled, exactly as she had last seen him three weeks before.

"I am so sorry, my dear," he said. "I fear I forgot again and went out for a walk without my goloshes."

"Henry!" she cried, and embraced him. "Where have you been?"

"Been?" He looked vaguely surprised, a little troubled. "Why—to tell you the truth I can't quite remember. But it will come back in time I hope—I devoutly hope." He looked wistfully round the familiar kitchen. "I see you were just about to make some cocoa, my dear. A cup of cocoa would be most welcome."

Miss Dallas wiped her eyes and set her trembling lips together. She had him back, and safe, that was the main thing. If she never discovered where he had been—why, it could not be helped.

"You are *sure* your feet are not wet, Henry? Why, what curious yellow stuff all over your shoes—it looks like down, or pollen."

"So it does," he said, staring at his shoes with a puzzled frown. "Where can it have come from? Ah, thank you, my dear. Cocoa—most acceptable and sustaining."

"Well, it's very nice to have you back, Henry," his sister said gruffly. "I was a little worried. However, it's over now. What would you say to a nice game of Twenty Questions?"

The Story about Caruso

No sooner had Uncle Roger gone to bed than Loraine, almost mechanically, jumped up out of her armchair, went into the kitchen, and started wolfing down cold suet pudding left over from supper.

It was lumpy, stodgy, cold, nauseating. Why was she eating it? She hardly knew. To make it go down at all she had to ladle on spoonfuls of jam. At last, sick, satiated, feeling as if she could not eat again for days, she returned to the fire.

Thank God, Uncle Roger turned in early, chirping about his beauty sleep. Night after night the same. "Well, Lorry, time for an old man's beauty sleep. Keep me roses in me cheeks!" A wink, a comic convulsion of his features, and the door closed on him, leaving Loraine with two, three, four hours in which the flat was her own again (except for the spare room and his shattering snore, punctual as a lightship's signal). But just the same, how, how, *how* was she going to get through the next ten years?

Or the next fifteen?

Of course he was getting on, of course, as her friend Cynthia had gaily, pityingly said, he wouldn't last for ever. But in the meantime there was his morning salute, on the dot of nine o'clock every day as he came out of his room, "Good morrow, mistress Lorry. How does your garden grow?"

There were his piteous, ineffectual efforts at housework while she was at her office every morning, his mangled, bungled apology for lunch—which he insisted on making. "You make the dinner at night, Lorry; *I* make the lunch. Fair 'do's,' eh?"

A lot of what Uncle Roger said went in inverted commas, clearly audible in his voice. He came of a generation that used slang with conscious and daring abandon.

"I've made a 'spiffing' soup, Lorry, me dear; I think you'll find that it's a real 'wowser.' Onions, carrots, kidneys, and just a dash of 'Woosh'; just a touch of Worcestershire sauce."

Uncle Roger was actually Loraine's husband's uncle. But during Rodney's lifetime they had seen little of him; Rodney had not been one for family ties. It was only after his death, and after Aunt Alice's death, that Loraine had felt obliged to offer a home to the old man. What else, indeed, could she do? He was over eighty, with no one to care for him and no pension, because he fell into some miscellaneous, in-between, uncatered-for-by-public-welfare group; he had spent all his capital; he had a weak heart; he could not be left on his own.

Against this, the weak heart had been with him for the last forty years, and Loraine honestly felt that she would go stamping, screaming crazy if she had to share her flat with him for another ten years, or ten months, or ten weeks. . . .

She had not been back sitting by the fire for more than five minutes when she sprang up as if jerked by a wire, hurried to the kitchen, ferreted in the back recesses of a cupboard, got out a half-bottle of whisky which had stood there untouched for the last nine months and, with reluctant, fascinated distaste, poured most of it into a tumbler and drank it down undiluted.

Why did I do that? she asked herself wonderingly. I didn't want it. I don't like whisky. It doesn't even cheer me up. Is it in order to feel I'm doing something independent of Uncle Roger? Something he doesn't know about? How stupid can one get?

I must control myself. I must take a grip.

Just the same, half an hour later, she was back in the kitchen, finishing the whisky and ravenously bolting down half a bar of unsweetened cooking chocolate; this in spite of the fact that the dinner she felt obliged every night to cook for Uncle Roger, who had a hearty appetite, was four times the size of her own normal evening meal.

I won't buy any more whisky, Loraine resolved next day. To make certain she kept her resolution she left all her money at home when she went to the office, leaving herself only enough for fares. Despite this, on the way home she went into the off licence, cashed a cheque, and bought two bottles of Cutty Sark.

"Topping tiffin today," chirped Uncle Roger, beaming at the head of the stairs as she walked up with her carrier bag. "Rissoles, made my special way—you'll love 'em, Lorry—and rice, and Harvard beets, and zabaglione. Aunt A always loved my zabaglione. A tour de force, she used to say. A real toower de force."

The kitchen was a shambles of blue smoke, egshells, soot, onion peel, and cigarette ash. Loraine with a physical effort restrained herself from picking her Irish-linen teacloths off the floor, where they were lying in a puddle of coffee grounds. She smiled at the old man and, as she could think of nothing to say, hurried through to her bedroom to take off her coat.

After the meal, and after the washing up, which Uncle Roger left to her because, as he said, "You know where everything goes, Lorry; and anyway I did the cooking—fair 'do's,' eh?" she munched chocolate savagely on her bed for five minutes, before leaving and catching the bus back to her office.

Uncle Roger had told several of his stories during lunch: the story of how he had met Bernard Shaw (second time of hearing); the story of how he sued the railway company and got compensation (third time of hearing); the story of how as a small boy he had been brought downstairs to hear a song recital by Caruso and what he had said (fifth or possibly sixth time of hearing).

After the chocolate Loraine also had a slug of whisky.

I must be fair, she said to herself, hurrying for her bus as if devils were after her. He has nothing in life now but memories, so naturally he offers them to me; they are his share of the housekeeping, his contribution towards entertainment. And naturally he wants to feel that those vivid passages of his life are still of interest, still important. (And actually, she acknowledged, they are interesting; if I read them in some book of memoirs I should be pleased to know what Bernard Shaw had said, what Southend Beach was like in 1890, what ladies wore for evening parties, what you did with your visiting cards, how you mounted a penny farthing.)

So why can't I take it from Uncle Roger?

I must stop eating chocolate; I've put on a stone since he came to live at the flat. I won't buy any today. I won't even leave the office until after the shops are shut.

She stayed in the office, doing extra work, catching up on long-term jobs, until half-past six, and then put shillings into three different automatic machines until she found one that worked, and wolfed the resulting chocolate bars in the kitchen while making supper. Uncle Roger was listening to a comedy programme on the radio, turned up so that he could hear. At supper he told her all the best lines.

Loraine could not be sure when the idea of murder first crawled into her mind. There was no financial gain associated with the thought—though Uncle Roger often gaily told her that all he had would be hers. In fact, she knew that his annuity died with him, and that his effects consisted principally of his Masonic regalia, some fishing tackle, a number of china souvenir vases, and half a dozen books on spiritualism.

Murder would not be for concrete gain. It would merely be for peace, for beautiful vanished peace, for household articles in their proper places and a chance to listen to radio concerts without interruption.

Killing him would be so easy. Every night at nine when he went to bed Uncle Roger took a sleeping pill.

"Have to, me dear," he confided to Loraine. "Me mind is so frighteningly active, you see! Without the pill I'd lie awake the whole blooming night, thinking of things to do which I'm too old to tackle. It would be plumb intolerable. So I got me doctor to prescribe some stuff that'll put me off to sleep without being too drastic on the old heart."

In fact, as Loraine had learned from the doctor when she took on Uncle Roger, the pills consisted largely of sugar and faith.

"So long as he believes in them they're quite enough to send him off. All you have to do is see he never gets hold of anything a grain stronger."

So there it was.

Loraine herself suffered from severe insomnia, and ever since Rodney died had been taking pills that were considerably more than a grain stronger than those prescribed for Uncle Roger. What could be simpler than the substitution of one for the another?

The day after this idea came into her mind she took her own supply of tablets and dropped them off Waterloo Bridge; thereafter she lay awake at night. Sometimes she thought about the pathos of an eighty-year-old man wishing to do all the things his age forbade.

It was on an evening when Loraine had some of her own friends in to dinner and Uncle Roger told them the Bernard Shaw, train, and Caruso stories in rapid succession, besides his warm opinion of what a grand little worker and housekeeper Lorry was, that events came to a head.

The friends had left. Uncle Roger had pottered off, considerably later than his usual retiring hour, to take a bath. "I know it's nothing but a bore me duffering about the kitchen putting your pots away in the wrong places, me dear!" Loraine was washing up. The water belched in boiling gusts out of the tap because, although frequently reminded, Uncle Roger had forgotten to switch off the immersion heater after he had washed his socks that morning.

Deliberately Loraine let the kitchen tap run. This, as she well knew, diminished the flow in the bath tap next door to a trickle.

Deliberately she waited until she heard, through the thin partition, Uncle Roger lower himself with grunts and gasps into his half-full, not too hot, nightly bath. Then she turned off the kitchen tap with a sharp flick of the wrist, imagining, as well as hearing, the resultant torrent that burst with scalding velocity out of the bath tap.

"Loraine!" screamed Uncle Roger. "Loraine! Help—"

She waited a minute, then slowly moved into the passage. She tried the bathroom door. She had often suggested that it might be wiser to leave it unlocked. But it was locked.

"Uncle Roger?" she called, with her face close to the panel. "Are you all right, Uncle Roger?"

But he didn't answer. All she could hear was the roar from the red-hot tap.

Loraine went to the telephone and dialed 999.

"Can you send police and an ambulance?" she said calmly.

Then she replaced the receiver, lifted up the divan mattress, pulled out a half-pound bar of raisin milk chocolate, and began eating it with controlled, absent-minded haste.

The Rented Swan

"This, you know, will not do," said Edwin Luffington. "It will not do at all." He gazed distastefully at the arched brick roof, from which a greenish drip occasionally fell to the floor. "My dear David (I may call you David?), we must get you out of here."

"Why? I've been here for a year. It's handy."

"It is quite unsuitable for a man in your position."

David Glendower looked at Edwin vaguely and then, a good phrase suddenly occurring to him, returned to his writing. There was nothing particularly striking about his immediate position; he was seated on two orange crates and making use of two more as a desk. His room, an enclosed arch under a viaduct in Kentish town, was neatly furnished with a series of shelves piled high with manuscripts, and a bed, all constructed from more orange crates; at two shillings a box they must have represented some five pounds' worth of outlay. The floor was muddy.

"Do you live here *all the time?*" pursued Luffington.

"Oh, no. I go to the castle in Wales for the summer months."

"Castle?" Luffington's expression perceptibly brightened.

"Pwllafftheniog. My ancestral home. I don't stay there in the winter because it's rather inaccessible; people won't deliver groceries." Reminded of food, he took another spoonful from a packet of mixed raw rice and currants which stood on his desk. "It's a day's ride from the nearest village."

"On what?"

"Donkey."

"Could you be photographed at the castle?"

"I *could*, I suppose. If it was a fine day. There are only two rooms with ceilings, and they leak a bit. . . . That's why I like this place. It reminds me of home."

"What's the rent?"

"The castle belongs to me. Oh, you mean here? Five shillings a month."

"You can afford more, now. How long has *A Nice Drop of Rain* been running?"

David glanced at a grubby theatrical poster and calculated on his finger.

"Ten months."

"And *The Night Sky in May* opens next week?"

"I believe so. Really I must hurry up and finish *Chips in Coromandel.*"

"And we've only just found out where you live," said Luffington, who represented an impressive firm of literary and theatrical agents. "Really Mr. Glendower—David—you keep yourself rather too well hidden away. Weren't you even interested to discover the amount of your bank balance?"

"I don't seem to need money much."

Luffington peered at him with disapproval. "You must get a new suit. And a new flat. Don't you understand, people want to meet you?"

"I haven't time to hunt for flats. I'm just at the crucial point in the second act. People must take me as they find me. But I'd rather they didn't find me."

"As to flats, you need have no worries at all, " Luffington said firmly. "There isn't any need to hunt. Another of our authors is abroad at the moment and I happen to know hers is available, furnished, on a year's lease. It will suit you admirably: a ground-floor flat in Curzon Street with a garden. And the rent is well within your present means. You can move in tomorrow; I will come here at ten with the office Bentley and help you move—you appear to have very little luggage—"

"I hope there will be room for my shelves; I don't want my manuscripts to get into a muddle."

"No there will *not*." Luffington cast a disparaging glance at the boxes. "But I can assure you the flat is *amply* furnished with cupboards, desks, and bureaus. And I myself will help with the manuscripts."

"There are forty-nine plays and seven sonnet sequences," David warned him.

Even Luffington's calm wavered for a moment, and the vaulted ceiling swam before his eyes in a superimposed vision of forty-nine box-office successes.

"How old did you say you were?"

"Twenty-five."

"And *A Nice Drop of Rain* was the first piece of work you sent out?"

"Yes; this flat you speak of"—David's tone was apprehensive—"I'll have to keep it dusted and so on?"

"Don't worry about *any* of that. The butler goes with the lease. He'll take care of you."

"Butler?"

"An old family retainer. The flat belongs to Louise Bonaventure—you've heard of her, I suppose?" Even you, his tone suggested, but David looked vague.

"She's an extremely well-known ornithologist. You must have seen her TV programmes—no, I suppose you may not have," he added as his gaze trailed down the damp walls to the candle in its saucer. "She travels in remote countries looking for rare birds. Her programme is called *Parlour Treks*. She's off on Whitsun Island at the moment, I believe. A delightful creature; you must meet her next year when she gets back." David looked mulish. "That's all, I think," Luffington ended briskly. "Till tomorrow then."

He departed, a willow-thin young man, wearing the very latest collarless haddock-skin jacket, with eyes as cold and intelligent as panel lights.

David went back to his writing and in two minutes had forgotten the visitor. The flat in Curzon Street was furnished and carpeted in the most elegant taste, but David, next day, hardly took it in, beyond noticing tiers of well-filled bookshelves with absent approval. Sitting down at a large, comfortable desk, he pulled out a pencil and notebook from his pocket, and had to be forcibly dragged away by Luffington to meet the lawyers and sign the lease.

Luffington rapidly read the document aloud. "Property on the ground floor of number tiddle-tum three, Curzon Street, hereinafter known as The Property, together with all fixtures, furnishings, fittings, appurtenances, trum, trum, trum, shall be . . ." David's attention drifted away. Could Luffington really have read "live and dead stock" or was that a phrase dimly recollected from the long-ago day when Glendower senior was sold up as bankrupt? "Subject to quarterly inspection by lessor or lessor's agents, trum, trum, trum . . . shall retain the services of HENRY WADSWORTH OGLETHORPE as butler at a salary of not less than . . . lease shall be subject to approval of hereinbeforementioned HENRY WADSWORTH. . . ."

"Just a formality," little Mr. Glibchick, the lawyer, was murmuring. "Miss Bonaventure was anxious to ensure that the flat should be sublet to someone, as she put it, on the same *wavelength* as herself. (The ladies, bless them, have these fancies.) She places the utmost reliance on the judgement of Oglethorpe—butler since she was a child."

"I have to be approved by this Oglethorpe?" David came back from Act II with an effort.

"If you don't mind, sir—"

"Where is he?"

"In the kitchen. I'll just—"

"I'll go myself. Through here?" David laid his finger in the notebook and folded Act II round it.

A plump, fatherly man sat at the spotless table oiling a seventeenth-century musical box. His face was platter-shaped and pastry-coloured, with shrewd, friendly eyes.

"You are Henry Wadsworth Oglethorpe? Good morning. I understand you have to approve me. If you'll just excuse me a moment—" David said politely, and wrote half a dozen lines, raising his head to say, "My name's David Glendower."

"Mr. Glendower, the playwright? You needn't have troubled, sir." Oglethorpe went placidly on with his task. "Miss Bonaventure has a very high opinion of you and so have I; I've seen your play twice."

"Oh, well, that's fine then. Very glad to make your acquaintance. What a beautiful musical box."

"Miss Louise collects them, sir. Would you care to hear it play?"

It played "Can Ye Sew Cushions" very sweetly and hauntingly.

"I know the words to that," said David, and supplied them in an agreeable tenor. Oglethorpe unexpectedly added the bass, and when, after twenty minutes, Luffington and Glibchick came in search, they had worked their way through to the "Ash Grove," with falsetto cadenzas by David.

The lease was signed, and the two men of business took their leave, Luffington promising to return and escort David to a tailor.

"Before you do that, sir, I'll get Mr. Glendower something off the peg," Oglethorpe suggested, measuring David with his eye, "for he can't be seen in Padrith and Kneale in *that* suit. And," he added, as the front door closed behind Luffington, "in the meantime, how about a nice hot bath, sir? While you're having it, I'll just pop out and get the suit—a Lovat I think would be suitable, Mr. David—and then I'll bring up a light, early lunch, shall I, and you can get straight on with your writing. An omelet and a bottle of Haut-Brion?"

"All right—" said David, steered neatly and inexorably in the direction of the bathroom. The hot water was already running. He felt vaguely that he was being remoulded, but since the process could not possibly upset his interior self, he did not particularly mind; in Oglethorpe's capable hands it was rather comfortable. Certainly a hot bath was a luxury he had not experienced for years, and quite acceptable, though he found Miss Bonaventure's bathroom, with its swansdown etceteras, dark-green marble, and sunk bath, alarmingly sybaritic.

Halfway through his bath, as he lay idly pushing the soap about with his toe and trying over lines of dialogue aloud (acoustically the room was superb), something rather disconcerting occurred.

A flash of movement caught his eye from a carved alabaster bracket by the window, on which reposed what he had taken to be a carved alabaster swan with its head tucked under its wing. Turning rather sharply, he now saw that the swan had thrust its neck forward, so that the head just protruded from under the wing, and was regarding him with a black and inscrutable eye.

David started so violently that a tidal wave slopped over the edge of the bath. Swans are baleful and unpredictable creatures at best, even when viewed from the vantage point of rowboat or towing path; to meet a swan when oneself recumbent, unclad, immersed, and on a much lower level is an unnerving experience. David glanced towards the bathroom door, gauging his distance, but the swan forestalled him by spreading a pair of wings with an eight-foot span and gliding to a point midway between bath and door. There it settled, tucking its flappers neatly underneath, curving its neck into a meticulous S-bend, and fixing its flat eyes on David.

With such an audience there was no pleasure in further soaking. Indeed, it seemed alarmingly possible that the bird might elect to share his bath with David. He dried himself hastily. Oglethorpe had removed his clothes and left him a towelling robe which afforded highly inadequate protection against swan assault. However, this bird's manner, though watchful, did not appear to be hostile. When David gingerly skirted round to reach the door, it swivelled its head, keeping the flat black eyes trained on him like AA guns, but allowed him to leave in an orderly manner.

He found Oglethorpe laying out the new suit, together with socks, underwear, shirt, tie, and handkerchief, all selected with severely professional discrimination as suitable to the image of a rising young playwright.

"Oglethorpe."

"Yes, Mr. David?"

"What is that swan doing in the bathroom?"

"It seems to like it in there, sir, when the weather's chilly. I suppose it's natural; the presence of water, you know, and the radiators. If you will not be requiring another bath this afternoon, I'll fill it with cold (adding just a dash of warm); it serves nicely as an indoor paddling pool."

"But what is the swan doing here *at all?*"

"It's in the lease, sir; didn't you read it? Furniture, fittings, appurtenances, and one swan, care of aforesaid swan to be undertaken by the hereinaftermentioned Henry Wadsworth Oglethorpe."

"I have to share this flat with a swan?"

"It is a very valuable bird, sir." Oglethorpe's tone held a faint touch of reproof. "A gold-banded swan of Izbanistan."

"Why isn't it at the zoo?"

"That wouldn't do for it at all, sir. It's a very particular bird."

"Bad-tempered?"

"Oh, I wouldn't say so, Mr. David." Was there a hint of reserve in his manner? "Keeps itself to itself, in general. When the weather's fine, of course, it will be in the garden."

David now understood why the garden, a pleasant little court with a grape arbour and fig tree, was three-quarters filled with an evidently new pool.

"What sex?" he asked. "The swan? Male or female?"

Oglethorpe answered repressively that the bird was a pen, and folded David's handkerchief into a neat geometrical figure. "I'll bring your lunch in ten minutes, Mr. David."

The omelet was delicious and the wine mellow; nevertheless, lunch would have been a more cheerful meal if the swan had not chosen to trundle, slowly and with dignity, into the dining room, where it sat on the serving cart, following the progress of every bite into David's mouth. He tried a placatory offer of toast fingers, which were ignored.

Hurrying back to work in the study, he heard slow, flapping footsteps behind him. Then there was a slight flurry, and Oglethorpe's voice, low, but firm: "Mr. David is busy with his writing and doesn't want to be bothered. I'll fill the bath and you can have a nice swim."

Feeling rather a pig, David closed the study door. Halfway through the afternoon (Act II was not going well) he felt obliged to tiptoe along to the bathroom and peer through the crack of the door. The swan was in the bath, sailing about above her reflection, and preening her back with brisk, housewifely jabs of the beak. She seemed contented enough, but was there a slight droop to her neck, as if she knew she had been rebuffed? Conscience-stricken, David left the study door open, and not long after kept his head assiduously bent over his notebook as a slow slipslop crossed the rush matting behind him. (Had she dried her feet before leaving the bathroom?)

At seven Oglethorpe, gliding in to inquire about the evening meal, found the playwright scribbling away like mad, while the swan, silent, impassive, but not unsympathetic, sat on a corner of his desk, pinning down a large heap of manuscript.

"I've made a casserole, sir. When would you like it?"

"I'd like it now," said David, stretching his cramped hand. "I've done enough."

When Oglethorpe brought the after-dinner coffee, David asked the swan's name.

"Miss Lou— that is, she hasn't exactly got a name, sir. Miss Louise never thought to name her."

"She ought to have a name. I shall call her Lucy Snowe," said David, thinking of the memorable descriptive sentence in *Villette*: "I, Lucy Snowe, was calm." Calmness seemed to be this Lucy's forte.

"Very good, sir. Shall you be wanting anything more?"

"No. Thank you, Oglethorpe. You're making me very comfortable," David said, looking from the peacefully glowing fire to the swan on the ebony concert grand with her head tucked under her wing. It was surprising how quickly one became accustomed to the presence of a swan in the room.

"It's a pleasure to look after you, sir." Oglethorpe gently closed the door, leaving the silent pair to their own reflections.

A week passed. Hounded by Luffington, David acquired a correct wardrobe, had a haircut that brought into view his haggard good looks, and attended the first night of his new play. It was an instant success.

With two plays running, David Glendower became a celebrity and, if Luffington had had his way, would have appeared at countless public occasions and TV interviews. David, however, had a strong faculty of self-preservation, which, backed by Oglethorpe's quelling manner of answering the telephone or door, kept most of his admirers at bay.

One of them got through, however.

Everyone who knew Blair Lanaway described her as a horrible girl, "but," they were obliged to add, "she does have staying power." It was true, she had. To this, and not at all to the fact that she was a Hon. did she owe her job as gossip columnist for *Fancy* magazine; she always got the copy she was after and it was universally admitted that she wrote the liveliest, knowingest, bitchiest column in the busines. She had a round face with pink pushed-up cushiony cheekbones, plum-black eyes, and a golliwog mop of black hair; her loud laugh and her ringing public-school tones were known from one end of Mayfair to the other end of Fleet Street.

The moment she laid eyes on David all her acquisitive instincts came into play.

David had the misfortune to twist his ankle slightly coming down the theatre steps after a compulsory visit to the three hundredth night of *A Nice Drop of Rain.* Blair happened to be at hand, she swooped on him like a hen harrier and insisted on driving him home in her nasty little car before he could extricate himself. Politeness demanded that he ask her in for a drink. As a matter of fact, Miss Lanaway practically carried him over the threshold, to Oglethorpe's evident and deep disapproval.

Before David could think of an excuse, she had invited him to dinner at her flat the following night, promising to come and fetch him.

In years to come when David woke, twitching from nightmares, he would remember that evening. Blair served him a hellish cocktail (he thought it might have been petrol and rosehip syrup with a pinch of phenobarbitone) ; thereafter he sat in a state of stupor. Blair curled herself up on the hearthrug and chattered gaily, but as the evening progressed she moved closer and closer until her elbows were on his knees and she was gazing intensely into his eyes; by about midnight she was saying with a boyish laugh, "Why bother to go home? I'll blow up the airbed if you prefer to sleep single."

"My butler will be worrying about me," David managed to articulate, trying to edge towards the door on his good foot.

"Bother your butler."

"And so will Lucy."

"Who's Lucy?" she said sharply.

" 'A maid whom there were none to praise, and very few to love.' Thanks for a delightful evening," he said, finding the doorknob as thankfully as a drowning swimmer finds a rock.

She was so annoyed that she let him go, and he managed to weave and hobble to the taxi rank.

But the following evening she called at the flat in Curzon Street. As ill luck would have it, Oglethorpe was out; it was his evening off and he was singing with the Aeolian choir in Haydn's *Creation*. David had to answer the door.

Blair surged past him, all generous sympathy, crying out, "You poor dear! Do you feel terrible after last night? Never mind, I forgive you! I've brought a bottle of Volga Dew for a pick-me-up. Don't trouble to hunt for a corkscrew; you sit down and rest your foot. I'm a champion at finding things in other people's kitchens. No Lucy? I knew you were pulling my leg."

"She's in the garden," David said faintly.

"*Nonsense*, sweetie, you're just a great big *storyteller*, aren't you? Here we are, clever little Blair's found two tumblers and a corkscrew, so let's be cosy."

David looked longingly towards the study, where Act II was waiting, but he did not know how to evict his unwelcome guest. He wondered how long it would be before Oglethorpe came home.

Blair had kicked her shoes off and would have let her hair down had it been possible. "Let's sit on the sofa," she said. "Now I want to talk to you about *contact*, David; for a man in your position, *contact* is so essential."

People always seemed to be lecturing him about his position, David thought; at the moment it seemed to be deteriorating alarmingly; he felt homesick for the viaduct.

At this moment three loud raps sounded on the window. Blair shot upright, greatly startled.

"Oh, that will be Lucy." David's tone was full of relief. "I expect she wants her bath mat."

He opened the window and laid in front of the fire a thick square of red towelling. Lucy hoisted herself over the sill and stalked forward onto the mat, where she carefully dried each flipper in turn. While she did so, she kept her head turned and her eyes trained on Blair; it seemed to David that there was something of definite malignity in the look she was directing at the visitor.

Blair felt this too. She paled. "I—I don't go for swans much," she said nervously. "Of course it's *too* marvellously brilliant and amusing of you to keep one for a pet—we *must* get some shots for *Fancy*—but couldn't it sit in the kitchen or somewhere?"

"Goodness, no. Lucy always sits with me. I wouldn't for worlds hurt her feelings."

"What about my feelings?" demanded Blair angrily. "Am I supposed to sit here with that bird staring at me?"

"Don't stay if you don't want to, of course," David replied courteously. Lucy abetted him by choosing at this moment to move slowly towards Blair with outthrust neck, emitting a low but meaningful hiss which had a completely routing effect. Blair left precipitately, with many reproaches, and David was able to return to Act II, while Lucy settled on the arm of his chair and dangled a contented length of neck over his shoulder.

It became plain that as a chaperon Lucy was unrivalled. On several subsequent occasions she rescued David from similar predicaments, and once she dealt with a pair of burglars who had been tempted by the valuable collection of musical boxes, breaking the leg of one and stunning the other, with a neat right-and-left of her powerful wings, before David and Oglethorpe had even woken up. In fact, Lucy became almost as much of a celebrity as her temporary owner, and featured with him in many a double spread.

Two months passed peacefully and productively by. January, however, brought a severe cold spell, with concomitant power cuts and fuel shortages. David, hardened by years under the viaduct, hardly felt the weather, but Lucy and Oglethorpe both suffered acutely and caught colds with distressing frequency. Oglethorpe nevertheless continued to look after David solicitously, while his care for Lucy was touching; he made her gargle—a process by no means easy for swans—night and morning, fed her vitamin capsules by the handful, and, when necessary, helped her to inhale steaming turpentine, sitting with her under the towel to ensure her compliance. One evening, fancying she looked a little pink round the eyes, he went out in the snow to procure her some tincture of cinnamon, and this was his undoing; he caught a bad cold which turned to pneumonia, and the doctor insisted on his removal to hospital. He protested vehemently.

"Don't worry, *please* don't worry," David exhorted him. "I'll look after everything here; you just concentrate on getting better."

"Miss Lucy—you'll look after Miss Lucy?" begged Oglethorpe.

"If anything happened to her I just don't know what—" His voice broke, and he was obliged to turn his head away on the stretcher.

"I'll do everything you did, I swear," David assured him. "Vitamin C, black-currant purée, quinine, hotwater bottle, the lot."

For a week all went well. Then, when the thermometer had shot down to twenty-six degrees, there was a forty-eight-hour power cut. The temperature in David's flat gradually sank to an arctic low, frost glistened on the walls, the bath froze (Lucy's outdoor pool had frozen long before). For the first day David managed to keep himself and Lucy warm by burning coal dust and branches stolen from Green Park, and filling hotwater bottles from kettles boiled on a spirit stove. On the second evening Lucy sneezed twice, and David noticed that she had begun to shiver. He filled an extra bottle and wrapped an eiderdown round her, but she shivered still, and he stared at her in worried perplexity. It was plain that she must not go through the night in such a state.

The solution he finally adopted seemed the only one possible. He piled all the bedding in the flat on his own bed, put all the hotwater bottles into it, administered an immense tot of brandy to Lucy and took one himself, then, grasping her firmly round her feathery middle, he wriggled into bed and went to sleep. It occurred to him drowsily in the middle of the night that he should have done this sooner; their combined warmth, and Lucy's feathers, produced an almost tropical temperature under the layers of quilt and blanket.

When he woke next morning he looked beside him on the pillow expecting to see black beady eyes and an elegant red bill. Instead, to his astonished dismay, he found an unmistakably feminine profile: that of a fair-haired, distinguished woman whom, if he had been a student of television, he would have recognised as Louise Bonaventure.

She opened her eyes and regarded him sleepily.

"How do you do?" she said. "I'm your landlady."

He pressed his knuckles to his forehead. "How did you get here?" he asked.

"It's a long story." Louise stretched luxuriously. Then she sat up and stepped briskly out of bed. "Let's have some coffee first, shall we? Is the power on again? Yes, thank goodness. How delicious coffee smells—it must be a year since I tasted it. Oh, you want to know how I got here? I was the swan."

"*Lucy?* My Lucy Snowe?"

Miss Bonaventure had the grace to look a little conscious. "I suppose I should apologise. You see, I'd collected a pair of Abominable Snowgeese in the mountains of Izbanistan, and the Imam found out, and was annoyed about it, said I had no right to—ridiculous of him, they aren't at all rare, over there, common as starlings—so in revenge he purloined one of my pair, had me turned into a swan by his top lama, a very accomplished magician, and popped me into the crate instead. If it hadn't been for Oglethorpe, who very intelligently put two and two together, I should have ended my life in the London zoo."

"But what broke the spell?"

She blushed faintly. "It must have been the old Frog Prince solution. I hope you haven't caught my cold?"

"Ought I to marry you?" David asked diffidently.

She gave him a somewhat baffling glance, but merely remarked, "There's no obligation about it—except on my side. I really am extremely grateful to you, and you've been an admirable tenant."

"Shall you want the flat back now?" David felt very confused, and instinctively kept the conversation on a businesslike level.

"Not immediately." Miss Bonaventure's fine eyes flashed. "First I shall fly to Izbanistan for another snowgoose. I'm not going to be downed by that old trickster of an Imam. But first let's go to the hospital and visit Oglethorpe."

Oglethorpe's delight at the restoration of his mistress was touching to witness. Tears of joy stood in his eyes. "It makes me better just to see you, Miss Louise," he kept declaring. "And you won't go back to those unreliable foreign parts any more, will you, my dearie?"

"Only to get another snowgoose, Henry dear. I must have a pair."

"Then I shall come too," the old man declared. He overbore all objections, and insisted on her waiting until he was well enough to accompany her. Meanwhile she moved to the Curzon Hotel, but spent a good deal of time at the flat, where she and David maintained their pleasantly easy relationship.

Two weeks after the travellers had departed, David suddenly

realised how bereft he was without them: no Oglethorpe to sing duets with of an evening, no sage advice as to ties and shirts, no imperturbable barricade against the outside world, and worst of all, no Lucy Snowe. Only now did he understand how much he had come to need her cool and silent presence. Without her he could hardly write.

He sent a cable to catch her at Elbruz: WILL YOU MARRY ME?

She replied, YES, OF COURSE, DUNDERHEAD, BUT MUST FIRST SECURE SPECIMEN. MEET ME HERE ON RETURN FROM IZBANISTAN.

Overjoyed, David booked a flight. All his urge to write had come back, and he was able to complete two acts on the thirty-hour trip. By the time he reached Elbruz, he calculated, her mission would be accomplished and they could get married at the British Embassy.

He reckoned without the Imam of Izbanistan.

When he reached the Taj Mahal hotel, the first person he saw was Oglethorpe, who looked travelworn and harassed.

"Oh, Mr. David, how glad I am to see you!"

"Is Miss Louise back?"

"Yes, she's back, but—"

"Did you get the goose?"

"Yes, we got it, but—"

"What's the trouble? She's not hurt?"

"No, nothing like that, sir, but that old Iman's been up to his magical tricks again."

"Turned her into a swan? Well, we know how to deal with that now," David said.

"Yes, well, it's a bit worse, this time, Mr. David. However, you'd best come and see for yourself. I'm not sure how long the hotel management is going to stand for it."

He led the way by lifts and corridors to a bedroom door which shook and rattled as if some huge and formidably active creature inside were attempting to get out.

"You're sure you're game, Mr. David?"

"Of course I am. Open the door, man!" David exclaimed. He was pale but resolute.

So Oglethorpe opened the door. . . .

Safe and Soundproof

THERE she sat, pretty as a bumblebee with her gold eyes and brown hair, attracting even more attention than men with hydraulic grabs on building sites. She sat behind a sheet of plate glass in Dowbridges' window, at a desk that was all made of glass, and she had a mighty mirror behind her.

At her side was a dear little electric furnace, all in white, and on the desk was a guillotine, not the sort fed by tumbrils full of aristos, but a handy paper-cutting size. With this she was demolishing stacks and stacks of documents, cutting them into slivers like bacon and then turning them round and repeating the process crossways until she had a mound of confetti. When it was knee-high, she slid the whole heap into a plastic basket and shot it into the furnace.

Pile after pile of paper the furance wolfed down with the barest flicker of acknowledgment, and Roger Mauleverer, watching through the window, thought of pine forests in Sweden and Canada, vast stretches of spruce and redwood towering majestically in snow and sunshine, all destined to total extinction after this girl had done with them. He felt quite cross about it, for he liked trees. But he had to admit that the girl was very attractive.

Over her head, right across the plate glass, he could read the inscription:

CONFIDENTIAL RECORDS EFFECTIVELY
DESTROYED UNDER GUARANTEE

For the first two weeks that Ghita Waring sat in the window, her boss, who had a flair for publicity, tied a bandage over her eyes so that it was plain she couldn't read the documents she was chopping. But she cut her finger three times.

The following week he put her in dark glasses, but he had to admit that the gold eyes were a loss. So the fourth week he contented himself with a notice on the front of her desk:

SHE ONLY READS MUSIC;
YOUR SECRETS ARE SAFE WITH HER.

Ghita's old headmistress, who happened to pass by and see this, was very annoyed about it and complained that it was a poor advertisement for her school, but Ghita merely laughed and said she didn't mind; anyway, it was almost true. Though she added that she could read cookery books if the words weren't too long. She managed to conceal her really dangerous gift; if it had been discovered she would hardly have landed the job.

It was a never-failing pleasure for passersby to stop and watch her and wonder what she was cutting up now.

"That's a will," muttered Sidey Curtiss to Bill Brewer. "Bang goes the long-lost blooming heir. Now what's she got?"

"Might be an agreement. See the red seal?"

"There goes a confidential file; some bloke's past history smoking up the chimbley. Pity she couldn't chop up your record, Bill, eh? Just phone police headquarters and tell 'em to send it along in a plain van."

Bill took this bit of humour coldly. "Why not ask 'er to chop off your fingerprints while she's at it?"

A van drew up beside them, not a plain one. It was one of Pickering and Pumphrey's expensive-looking utilities. Beside the driver sat Miss Inglis, the gaunt, severe secretary of old Mr. Pumphrey himself. She got out of the van with dignity and marched inside, carrying a large roll of paper. She talked for a short time with the golden-eyed girl at the desk and then came out again, leaving the document behind her. She stepped back into the van and was buzzed away down to the immense and gleaming new office building that Pickering and Pumphrey had just erected at the other end of the square.

"Wonder what they're getting rid of?" speculated Sidey.

"Something old Pumphrey doesn't want to be blackmailed about," suggested Bill. "Cor, here comes a smasher." He stared approvingly at a sapphire-and-mink blonde who burst out of a taxi like a ray of sunshine coming out of a cloud. "Bet *she's* got some compromising letters."

The blonde sailed inside, and presently the two watchers saw her pull a bundle of letters from her magnificent handbag and pass them across to the girl at the desk. They saw her talking vigorously.

"It really does seem a shame to destroy them," was what she was saying. "They're so romantic. I can't bear for someone not to see them. You read them, ducky. You must get bored chopping away all the time and never a chance of a peep. And Roger's letters are as good as Shakespeare; they're so poetic they always make me cry. It's like murdering a child to have them guillotined." She dabbed at her eyes. "But he says I've got to. See, in the last letter."

Ghita looked at the top one. "*Dear Rosemary,*" it said baldly, "*in view of developments, please destroy all my letters. I am returning yours herewith.*"

"That's not very poetic, surely," Ghita said.

"Ah, but look at the earlier ones, ducky."

It certainly was rather a treat for Ghita to be allowed to read a document before destroying it, and she glanced at one or two of the letters towards the bottom of the pile. When she read them her golden eyes became larger and rounder and mistier.

"Why, they're beautiful," she breathed.

"Aren't they," said Rosemary with satisfaction. "I do miss him, you know. No one else has ever said such beautiful things to me." She dabbed her eyes again. "Oh, would you mind giving me a testimonial, or whatever you call it, saying you've destroyed them? Roger is so fierce, and he's been beastly enough to me as it is. I don't want any more trouble." Her lip quivered.

The man must be a brute, Ghita thought indignantly. Fancy writing letters like that to a girl and then making her destroy them; demanding it so curtly, too.

"I HEREBY CERTIFY," she wrote, "THAT I HAVE DESTROYED TWENTY HAND-WRITTEN LETTERS TO MISS ROSEMARY TRENCH-

GIDDERING FROM "ROGER," QUINCETREE COTTAGE, BROKEN END, HAZELDEAN."

Why, she thought to herself in sudden enlightenment, he must be the young architect that Mother's always talking about, who's taken Quincetree Cottage. I shouldn't have thought he'd been there long enough to write twenty letters. And then he asks her to destroy them. What a trifler! What a snake in the grass!

"That will be one pound, please," she said.

"Thank you, ducky," said Rosemary. She gave a last dab to her eyes, a lingering glance at the last letter coming under the headsman's axe. "Ah well . . ." She straightened her shoulders with a billowing glitter of mink, dazzled Ghita with her smile, and ran out to the taxi, which was still stolidly ticking up three pences.

"Now 'e won't be able ter prove a thing," muttered Sidey to Bill. The drama had gone out of the window, but they still lingered in the spring sunshine watching Ghita, who had pulled towards her the large scroll left by Miss Inglis.

Absently she scanned it, and then blushed pink as she realised that she had violated professional ethics. Being allowed to read Rosemary's letters had led her astray.

She glanced up, scowled at the two seedy watchers outside, and grabbed her guillotine. In her confusion she let the scroll slip and it rolled to the floor, displaying its contents. She pounced on it and minced it into ribbons as if it had bitten her. Anyway it was only a blueprint; no possible harm could come from her having glanced at it.

"Did you see what that was?" said Bill to Sidey. "It was the plans of Pickering and Pumphrey's new office building."

"Well, what of it?" said Sidey. "Come on, I'm getting cold. I want a cuppa."

"What of it, you daft fool, what *of* it? Why, don't you see? . . ."

He was talking urgently as they moved off to the Bide-Awile Café.

It was bad luck on Ghita that she had a photographic memory.

"Some people are coming in for drinks," Mrs. Waring said when Ghita went home on Friday. "That nice young Mr.

Mauleverer who's taken Quincetree Cottage will be here. I think I've mentioned him before."

"Only about forty times," said Ghita, but she said it to herself. She knew, and her mother knew that she knew, and she knew that her mother knew that she knew, that Mrs. Waring disapproved of Ghita's chopping documents by day in order to put herself through music school at night. Both these occupations were nonsensical, Mrs. Waring considered; the sort of fandangle that a girl who was engaged, say, to a nice young architect, would soon put behind her.

Nice young Mr. Mauleverer indeed, Ghita thought, hugging her mother affectionately. I could tell you a thing or two about that two-faced fiend in human form if I weren't a model of professional discretion. Just don't let him try his come-hither tactics on me, that's all.

Nice young Mr. Mauleverer had a somewhat familiar face. After a little thought Ghita identified him as the tall, dark young man who had passed by her shop window nine or ten or eleven times in the course of the last few days. So that's who you are, is it, she thought, and she gave him such a flash of her eye, along with one of her mother's walnut canapés, that he staggered as if he had been stabbed with an eighteen-carat tie pin.

"I hear you are studying music," he said, recovering. "I compose a little myself."

"Oh, do you?" Ghita said, interested in spite of herself. "What sort of things?"

"Songs," Roger Mauleverer said, and for some mysterious reason he chuckled. "I write songs."

The chuckle incensed Ghita. "I shouldn't think you had a great deal of time for writing songs," she said icily. "Writing letters must be such an engrossing occupation." She gave him a meaning look, and he eyed her warily.

"Am I to infer that my ex-fiancée has been to you professionally?"

"Miss Trench-Giddering has confided in me and has all my sympathy. But my lips are sealed," Ghita said firmly. And that's settled *him*, she thought with satisfaction. Now we know where we stand with each other.

She darted another disapproving, golden flash at him, was

pleased to see that it appeared to leave him quite prostrated, and went on to offer her walnut canapés with the utmost grace and charm to ninety-year-old Great Uncle Wilberforce.

On Wednesday, when Ghita was having her elevenses over the local paper, in between spells of guillotining, her satisfaction was given a jolt, and she was more than a little disconcerted to read a report of the wedding of Miss Rosemary Trench-Giddering to Mr. Cecil Quayle, M.P., with eight bridesmaids and all the trimmings. There were several photographs, and it was easy to see that Mr. Quayle, prosperous though he seemed—and as Ghita knew him to be, for he owned the town's largest factory—was about three times the age of the bride, who could hardly be seen behind the enormous diamond she wore.

Ghita began to feel a little contrite and remorseful. Lifting her eyes to the window, she thought that supposing, just supposing, Roger Mauleverer were to pass by, as he had done some eight or nine or ten times in the last few days, there would be no harm in giving him a friendly smile. But there was nobody outside the window except those two seedy-looking toughs who seemed to have spent a lot of time loitering round there lately.

She turned back to the paper, and a familiar name caught her eye: Roger Mauleverer, Associate of the Royal Institute of British Architects.

Roger Mauleverer, A.R.I.B.A., was, it appeared, the architect responsible for the large new office building recently erected in the town's main square on behalf of the local firm of Pickering and Pumphrey; the building had just been completed and the ceremonial tape cut by Mrs. Pumphrey, wife of the managing director.

An unusual feature of the building was the hidden safe-deposit room concealed on one of its nine floors. No one knew the whereabouts of this soundproof room except Mr. Pumphrey, Mr. Harris, the chief cashier, and the architect himself. Even the plans of the building had been destroyed so that unauthorised persons could not stumble on the information. The door of the room was opened by the newest form of electronic device; it would respond only to a code word spoken outside it. Needless to say, this code word was known to only four people: Mr. Pumphrey, Mr. Harris, the chief cashier, and the architect.

And to me, Ghita thought in cold horror. The type of the newspaper swam before her guilty eyes. Never, never, she thought, would she look at another document, however innocuous it appeared; no, not if fifty people begged her to on their bended knees. She knew now what that blueprint had been; she knew which floor the room was on, she knew which door led to it, and worst of all she knew, for it had been written in the margin, the code word that would open the door.

What ought she to do? Hasten to Mr. Pumphrey and tell him that his secret was discovered? Consult a psychiatrist and ask if there was any way of expunging the guilty knowledge from her mind? Or go to Roger Mauleverer and ask his advice?

Something about the simplicity of the last course commended itself. I'll ask him on Saturday, she thought—for her mother had artlessly invited him to Saturday supper. Nothing much can happen between now and then.

She was very, very wrong.

If she had read the Stop Press column in the evening paper, she would have seen the item headed MISSING MANAGING DIRECTOR. But she did not. She had a class on Diminished and Augmented Triads at half past six, and, hellbent to get to it, she thrust the evening paper in among her shopping and ran like a doe to the City Literary Institute in Tennyson Street.

It was late when she came out, late and dark and quiet. Tennyson Street, all foggy and cobbled, looked like a set from a French film, and it looked still more like one when two shadowy figures came up softly and menacingly behind Ghita and slipped a sack over her head. Her hands were tied behind her back and she was whisked into an alley that led, as she knew, to the river.

"Don't yell, *don't*," a hoarse voice said warningly in her ear, "because if you do we'll have to treat you rough. Just you keep quiet. We only want you to tell us something and then we'll let you go."

"What do you want?" Ghita gasped inside the bag. A cold premonition had already told her the answer.

"We was watching you the other day a-reading of a blueprint," the voice said ingratiatingly. "We saw your beautiful eyes a-taking of it in. All we want from you is the whereabouts of that there famous secret room at Pickering's what's got a million of di'monds shut away in it; and the code word for opening the door. That's all we want."

"I shan't tell you," said Ghita.

"Now, duck, don't you be so hasty. If you do tell us, who's to know it was you passed on the information? No one but us knows you read the plan. But if you *don't* tell us—"

"What?" Ghita said uneasily, for he had paused.

"Why, then I'm afraid we shall have to take you to the end of this alley and drop you in the river. Runs powerful fast the river does hereabouts," the voice said reflectively.

Ghita shivered. She had never tried swimming with her hands tied behind her back, but she didn't think she would excel at it.

An idea struck her. "I can't possibly explain where the door is," she said. "It's much too complicated. I can tell you the password. It's Lancashire Hot-Pot. Now will you let me go?"

"Not likely," said Sidey. "You'll have to come with us and show us. Once you get inside the building you'll know where you are. Coming? Or do we have to drop you in the water?"

"All right, I'm coming," Ghita said sadly. "The room's in the basement."

The route they took to Pickering and Pumphrey's was circuitous and entailed climbing some fences, crossing a bomb site, and cutting through a warehouse. At length they arrived in a wide, dark basement area next to a car park. Sidey, scouting ahead, picked a lock and let them in through a service door.

Ghita saw nothing of all this, for her head was still in the sack, but now they took it off and let her look round and get her bearings. Unerringly she led them along a red-and-white tiled corridor in which floated a haunting and evocative smell of stew. It ended at double red doors, chromium handled, and labelled DIRECTORS' CANTEEN. They were locked.

"Here you are," Ghita whispered. "That notice is a blind. It isn't really the canteen, that's on the first floor. Now you must stand here and say Lancashire Hot-Pot. But you have to say it in a particular tone of voice, and that's what I don't know, because I only saw it written down. You'll have to keep on trying till you hit the right pitch."

"Got it all pat, ain't she," Bill whispered admiringly. "You oughter come into the profession, miss; you'd do champion at it. Now then, Sidey, you try first, tenor and counter-tenor. Then I'll try bass and baritone."

"Lancashire Hot-Pot," said Sidey.

At about the twentieth attempt, when they were getting really enthusiastic, Ghita slipped quietly away round the corner to the little block where LIFTS had been marked on the ground plan.

Yes, here they were; and in such a modern building they were sure to be automatic. She pressed a button. Luckily they'd had to untie her hands to climb the fences. A lift came gliding down, and she tiptoed in and wafted herself up to the ninth floor, where, among other things, she remembered having noticed the switchboard room. Thank goodness, the police station was only a couple of blocks away!

But when she stepped out of the lift she was thunderstruck to find lights burning, footsteps clattering, and an atmosphere of hectic activity, very unexpected in an office building at ten minutes to midnight.

Three men hurried past her, distraught and preoccupied.

"Hey!" Ghita said. "There are two burglars in the basement, trying to get into the safe-deposit room."

"Those aren't burglars, my good girl," one of the men said testily. "The building's full of 'em. The managing director's got himself stuck inside the strongroom, and no one knows where it is. Everybody's trying to find him." Evidently he took her for a member of the staff.

"What about Mr. Harris, the chief cashier?" suggested Ghita, very much taken aback by this new development.

"He's having his spring week sailing in the Baltic."

"Well then, what about . . . ?"

But they hurried away, calling, "Throgmorton, Throgmorton, have you tried the mezzanine floor?"

"Wait!" Ghita called. She chased them and caught them at the head of the stairs. "I can tell you where the safe-deposit room is!"

"*You* can?" They turned and regarded her with suspicion. "How?"

"Well, never mind that for now," Ghita said. "It's on this floor, the fourth door to the right from the auditors' room."

By this time a group had assembled.

"I tried to get the architect, Mr. Throgmorton," someone said, panting. "I tried five times. But there's no reply from his number."

"This young person seems to think she knows where the door is," Mr. Throgmorton said with awful majesty.

Ghita's feelings of guilt and confusion intensified. She went trembling up to the fourth door and pointed at it. "That should be the one, and the password's Pickled Pumpkins."

Mr. Throgmorton gave her a look which, although she was ice cold with fright, chilled her still further. He placed himself directly in front of the door, looked at it commandingly, and uttered the words "Pickled Pumpkins" in a sonorous voice.

Nothing happened.

Ghita began to wish that she could fall down the lift shaft, or, failing that, just drop dead. She wondered what had gone wrong. And now that her password had failed, how was she ever going to introduce the topic of the two safe-breakers in the basement? But at that moment, she noticed that Roger Mauleverer was behind her.

"Ah, Mr. Mauleverer," Throgmorton said reprovingly. "It took you a very long time to get here."

"Long time?" Roger said, puzzled. "I came just as fast as I possibly could. Is Miss Waring all right?" He looked anxiously at Ghita.

"Miss Waring? I am not aware that she has been in any trouble. It is Mr. Pumphrey we are concerned with. Mr. Pumphrey is immured in the strongroom."

"Oh, is that all?" Roger said cheerfully. "We can soon get him out of there."

He stepped up to the door and serenaded it in a pleasing tenor:

"*Safe, my dear, list and hear!*
None but I is standing near."

This seemed an inaccuracy to Ghita, but everybody else was dead serious.

"None can pry, none can see,
Open wide your door to me."

The door swung open and revealed Mr. Pumphrey, indignant and ravenous, ensconced in a nest of diamonds and securities.

"I forgot the tune," he said accusingly to Roger. "That's the trouble with these fancy gimmicks!"

"Well, sir," said Roger, "it was your idea to have a tune. If you recall, I was in favour of the simple words Pickled Pumpkins, and it was you who said that you'd look like a fool if one of your staff found you in the corridor saying Pickled Pumpkins, and it would be better if you had a verse that you could sing."

"You must think of something else tomorrow," snapped Mr. Pumphrey. "Have to, anyway, now half the staff's heard it."

He glared round, explosive as a turkeycock. "Let alone this young lady, who's not a staff member. What's she doing here?"

"She told us where the strongroom was," Throgmorton said.

"What? How the devil did she know that?"

Trembling, Ghita confessed how she had come by her knowledge.

"I shall ring up Dowbridges," Mr. Pumphrey said, with the quiet menace of an impending avalanche. "That's the last of my business they handle. And what, pray, were you doing in my building at this time of night?"

"I was b-brought here by two burglars." Ghita faltered. "They're down in the basement saying L-Lancashire Hot-Pot outside the Directors' Canteen."

"I beg your pardon?"

But, thank heaven, Roger seemed to have grasped the situation. He murmured something to Throgmorton and the other two men. They shot away in the lift, found Sidey and Bill trying Hot-Pot for the seventy-seventh time in A alt and middle C, and nobbled them. The two burglars, hoarse and exhausted, were glad to go quietly.

"Where is Miss Waring?" Roger asked when they led the captives before Mr. Pumphrey, who had the telephone in his hand.

"She took her departure," Mr. Pumphrey said severely, "after I had issued her a warning." He put down the receiver.

Poor Ghita crept to her office next morning more dead than alive. Instead of the usual pile of documents awaiting destruction there was one envelope on her desk. It said, "Please read before destroying." Inside was a week's salary and notice of dismissal from her boss, who had been rung by Mr. Pumphrey at ten minutes past midnight.

Two large tears trickled down Ghita's cheeks and splashed on the glass desk. Absently she slid her notice into the guillotine and sliced it into spills. Then she looked up and saw Roger outside the window. She glared at him. Undeterred, he came in.

"It's all your fault," Ghita stormed at him. "If I hadn't been inveigled into reading your letters, I'd never have looked at that blueprint. And now I've got the sack, and I'll probably go to p-prison, and I'll never be able to afford to finish learning about Diminished and Augmented Triads, and what do *you* care?"

"I do care," Roger said. "Very much. I *love* Augmented Triads." Something about the way in which he said this, coupled with the fact that he was holding Ghita in a close embrace at the time, carried instant conviction.

He went on: "I explained to Mr. Pumphrey that you'd been shanghaied, and he says he's sorry he misunderstood the situation and he'll put it right with your boss."

"But how did you know about it?" Ghita said, wiping her eyes on his lapel, regardless of the interested spectators outside.

"I was lecturing on architecture at the City Literary Institute last night, and I looked out of the window and saw them putting your head in the bag. By the time I'd dashed out you were gone, but I guessed where they'd be making for."

"It was nice of you to bother," Ghita said, and added in a small voice, "I owe you an apology about Miss Trench-Giddering. Did you mind terribly when she married Mr. Quayle?"

"Frankly, no," said Roger, very cheerfully for a rejected suitor. "She was grand for practising my literary style on. But I wouldn't want to spend my life with somebody who sleeps all day and spends the hours between ten p.m. and five a.m. in half a dozen night clubs. I hate ear-splitting music."

Ghita drew back a couple of inches and looked at him nervously. "What about piano playing?"

"The minute we're married," he said, "I shall design us a house with a soundproof room in the middle, where you can pile up the Augmented Triads to your heart's content."

Cricket

THERE had been a persistent knocking from within the septic tank for several days, and by degrees it could not but become plain that someone must be trapped inside it.

The Beauclerks were too cautious, nay, parsimonious, to use anything for its rightful purpose; consequently the tank was employed as a storehouse for kilner jars, sugar soap, trunks, manuscripts of Christmas carols, and other things used only once a year. A distant portion of the orchard, known as the Belvedere, was allotted for the usual purpose of the w.c., which housed live bait.

Mrs. Beauclerk was sowing late peas in the hot afternoon sun when the Reverend Henry Dottel came weaving on his bicycle across the lawn.

"So like the powdered tomato soup, isn't it?" she said, straightening up and scratching her back with the dibber in a manner as dignified and archaic as that of a priest in a formal ritual. Mr. Dottel peered anxiously at the mixture of red lead and paraffin which she had in her saucepan. It did resemble tomato soup with a few dried peas rolling about in it, and he felt that Mrs. Beauclerk would be quite capable of serving it up at table.

"When you bury my husband you had better be sure to ask for an autopsy first."

The deep voice over his head made him jump. She had read his thought with disconcerting accuracy, and it was unfair that she should be so much taller than he; towering over his head, she was like some primitive African goddess.

"You want to speak to Fred, no doubt," she said, and indeed the Admiral was swinging himself across the garden in his chair, which was something between a flying fox and an overhead cash conveyor, slung from tree to tree.

"Do you want to discuss the match against Sleeve?" he asked eagerly as the chair came to rest under the Florence Court Yew. "You had better put Beeswick in to bat first. I've been thinking about it all night."

"No, I hadn't come about that." The Admiral's face fell. "My errand was of a more serious nature. I wanted to remind you once more that it is time little Daffodil was christened."

He had evidently screwed up all his courage to speak, but met with a blank reception; the Admiral was bored and disappointed, while his wife assumed a withdrawn, dispassionate air, and dropped a few more peas into her drill.

"That's really Jasper's affair," she remarked. "After all, he's her father."

"My son will see to it," the Admiral agreed. "Here he is."

The Hon. Jasper Beauclerk was as tall as his mother, but looked wild where she was patrician. He came prowling towards them, glancing from right to left as if only invisible palisades kept him from escaping.

"Mr. Dottel wishes to christen little Daffodil," his mother observed. She glanced in the direction of the converted pig trough where her grandchild lay kicking and cooing.

"No!" Jasper almost shouted.

"But, my dear boy! Supposing she were to contract polio or measles—unlikely eventualities, thank Providence, but such misfortunes do occur—how would you feel if she were to die without having been christened?"

"At least she'd be in the same place as her mother, wherever *that* is," snapped Jasper furiously and miserably.

"My son still feels his wife's loss very deeply," the Admiral apologised as Mrs. Beauclerk led Jasper aside and appeared to soothe and restrain him. "In a way it's a mistake, you know, marrying these Melanesian women. Marvellous cooks, of course,

I've never for one moment regretted marrying Lobelia, but some of them are too delicate for the English climate. And what's worse, they none of them take any interest in sport. I can't even get Lobelia to follow the Test Match, and Jasper takes after her, though I've done my best with the boy. There's precious little hope for Daffodil, having the strain from both parents."

Jasper and his mother had finished their colloquy and returned to the other two.

"Let's stroll down to the millrace, Mr. Dottel," said Mrs. Beauclerk. "It's cooler down there; we can discuss the matter more comfortably."

Jasper let out an inarticulate protest, but she hushed him with a gesture of calm authority.

The Admiral eyed them with suspicion as they crossed the sunbaked lawn.

"You must understand," Mrs. Beauclerk went on, "that my daughter-in-law's last wish was that the baby should *not* be christened. She belonged, as I do, to the Kiya religion, which, of course, is a form of sun worship."

"Rank heathenism," said Mr. Dottel, shuddering. "Some of them are cannibals, too, aren't they? Of course I don't mean to cast any aspersions at *you*, dear lady, though indeed, living in the Manor House as you do, it would be greatly appreciated if you were to attend morning service from time to time."

Mrs. Beauclerk gazed at him abstractedly. She might have been measuring him for a shroud.

"*Now*, I think," she said to Jasper as they crossed the narrow catwalk above the millrace, and seizing Mr. Dottel by his shoulders, she tipped him in. He went round in the swirl two or three times while Jasper, with a long pole, adroitly kept him from climbing out. After the fourth revolution he sank, and did not reappear.

"We still have a barrel of vinegar," observed Mrs. Beauclerk with satisfaction. "If you pour it in, he should keep nicely till Sunday."

At this moment a clanging and tingling of wires announced the furious advent of the Admiral, bearing down on them like an avenging angel.

"You've done it!" he said. "I thought you were up to something of the kind. Play these tricks on strangers, if you must, but now what the devil are we to do for a wicket keeper?"

"Oh, really, Fred, he was getting to be a terrible nuisance," remonstrated Mrs. Beauclerk. "You'll find somebody else to keep your wicket easily enough."

"Find someone indeed! Just tell me who, in this blasted countryside!"

"How about the person in the septic tank?"

"That's an extremely good idea," said the Admiral, brightening. "Of course it may be a woman," he added, relapsing into gloom. "Still, it's worth trying."

He swung his chair round and propelled himself feverishly in the direction of the manhole cover. The baby's improvised cot was on it, and it took a moment to move her aside, during which time the banging from beneath grew more excited and obstreperous.

The Admiral raised the thick metal cover and peered through the crack.

"Do you play cricket?" he bawled.

A faint reply came back. The Admiral let slip the lid, which fell into place with a clang.

"Hockey!" he said, with an expression of disgust, and climbed heavily into his chair.

Our Feathered Friends

MAJOR TEAPE was passionately fond of tidiness, had a perfect reverence for it. He was not very tidy himself, but he was logical and irascible, qualities which, he felt, made up for any little lack of complete order in his house. He and his dog, Rover, were so tall, so spare and uncheerful that his tenant, Miss Murdeigh, always felt a strong desire to snip a bit off them and put them in a vase of warm water with a penny in it, to revive them.

In money matters the Major was rigidly impeccable and on any day in the month could tell where his money was to the last halfpenny, not to mention the money in the organ fund, the brass-band takings, the men's club subscriptions, and the various separate accounts he himself kept in the local bank for poultry profits, rates, emergencies, and pocket money.

Naturally with all this his house was a bit untidy, for the machines were always breaking down and having to be repaired, so of course the dining-room table was covered with the components of the water softener, neatly arranged (the table was never used anyway) ; the diesel pump and lawn mower were in for repair too, but nevertheless *you could walk*, it was not like some people's houses. The engine that supplied the electricity was giving trouble too.

One could not be sure of finding a hammer in the Major's house, or a bit of fuse wire, or the pliers, without delving through four or five tables and workbenches covered with valves, spanners, springs, sparking plugs, and long oily bits of cable; but it was a dead certainty that in Miss Murdeigh's no hammer would ever be found at all, though the original score of an unpublished Haydn symphony might come to light. If Miss Murdeigh wanted to hammer in a nail, which was seldom, she did it with a brick; and she had no need for electricity, because she preferred candles.

The Major often said with restraint that Miss Murdeigh's house was very untidy, very untidy indeed.

His main cause for complaint against her was what he called her unreliability in money matters. She had been installed as his tenant in Orchard Cottage during the war, when the Major's back was, so to speak, turned; and when he had leisure to deal with her he found it impossible, simply impossible, to get her to understand that he wished his rent to be in *cash*, and not in any form that occurred to the inventive mind of Miss Murdeigh.

She frequently pointed out to him that he was the gainer in these transactions, since the actual value of a first edition, or an original Hogarth drawing, or three pounds of Jersey cream was more than the rent. Cash played a negligible part in her life. Subsisting as she did almost entirely off her smallholding, she found it much more convenient to pay him in kind; but the Major did not see eye to eye with her over this. He wanted tangible coins or notes that he could place in one of a series of cashboxes labelled Orchard Cottage Accounts, and he told Miss Murdeigh so, patiently, or fairly patiently, ever so many times.

"But honey is so good for you," Miss Murdeigh said in a mild tone, standing with the untidy greaseproof paper parcel in her hands. "I'm sure you don't get enough sugar into your system."

"Sell it to me, then," screamed the Major, at the end of his tether, "and pay the rent with the proceeds."

"Twelve and six, if you must, but it doesn't seem the same thing," she sighed, watching as he violently unlocked a cashbox labelled Poultry Profits and shovelled out five half-crowns. Four of them she handed back to him and he threw them into the Orchard Cottage box. "I wish to goodness," he said savagely as he put the keys in an envelope, "I wish to goodness you'd buy Orchard Cottage, and then I could get it out of my mind. I couldn't in decency ask more than two hundred for it, and I shall never be able to let it again. I suppose the roof is leaking, isn't it?"

"Do you suppose so?" said Miss Murdeigh vaguely.

"Bound to be. I'll send Hutton over on Monday."

"I don't think I could buy it," Miss Murdeigh went on, consideringly. "I very much doubt if I could do that. I have only seven pounds at present."

The Major made a gesture of despair, and Miss Murdeigh took her departure. But his remark bore fruit, for about a week later when he returned from Boy Scouts he found that his tenant had called while he was absent. On the kitchen table (his daughter, Sally, made him keep this clear) she had left a most extraordinary article—a glass dome, covering two of the shabbiest, seediest stuffed birds he had ever seen in his life, with lacklustre eyes and hardly a feather between them. They were seated on an elaborate erection something like the Albert Memorial, in attitudes of indescribably rakish abandon. At any minute, it seemed, they might burst into a dance.

A note in Miss Murdeigh's handwriting, propped against the glass case, said:

DEAR MAJOR TEAPE, *since our conversation last week I have been turning over in my mind the question of buying Orchard Cottage, and I have hit on this solution. My friend Constantia Lambrette, the harpist, who is staying with me at the moment, assures me that this set is worth at least five hundred pounds, and I therefore suggest that you take it in exchange for Orchard Cottage. It is an early and authentic piece by Liefmehr, in full working order, except that I have unfortunately lost the key. Pray accept the difference in price as a token of good-neighbourhood, and in requital for all the trouble I have caused you, and your many kindnesses.*

The Major nearly burst a blood vessel at this missive. He hardly waited to fling on his duffel coat again before stamping out with the early Liefmehr (it weighed a good ten pounds) clasped in his arms. But then he reflected that in five minutes it would be Rover's feeding time, so he slammed back again for two handfuls of dog biscuits, which he thrust into his pockets, and then once more set out for Orchard Cottage with Rover following at his heels.

What made it so much more annoying was that he had taken rather a fancy to the Liefmehr. He had a passion for alarm clocks—so long as they went. The house was full of dust-covered dead clocks and one or two large live ones, which tocked out solemnly the steps to eternity. (The small ones, somehow, never seemed to stand the strain for long.) And there were also pingers and chronometers, sundials and barometers; anything that went round was dearly liked by the Major. Plainly Miss Murdeigh's treasure was some sort of musical box, and the Major's fingers itched to investigate it. But the principles of an English gentleman and a landlord restrained him.

The path to Orchard Cottage lay, not surprisingly, through the orchard. The door was open but nobody seemed to be about. The Major went in and waited, restraining his disapproval with such an effort that he began to sweat slightly.

The brick floor was thick with dust. Two ghostly shapes, swathed in parachute nylon, were Miss Murdeigh's Bechstein and Miss Lambrette's harp. Narrow lanes led to them through the furniture, which was plentiful. A table by the window held manuscripts, matches, bits of sealing wax, shallots, garden tools, dirty plates and coffee cups, candlesticks, a Chianti bottle or two, embroidery catalogues, some Christmas cards, two bowls of narcissi, and piles of books. The Major ruthlessly swept these things to one side and set down his burden; then, consulting his watch, he called Rover and scattered the dog biscuits on the front doorstep.

Fuming, he sat down on an oak settle. He knew that his hostess could not be long, for it was nearly milking time and her two Jerseys were standing in the cabbage plot near the house; unmethodical Miss Murdeigh might be, but the Major knew that with her, consideration to animals was a creed. It was her only characteristic of which he wholeheartedly approved.

While he waited he heard a mysterious rumbling on the floor. At first he could not locate it. Could it be deathwatch? But no, it was too loud for that. Whenever he moved, it stopped.

At last he was able to trace it to one corner under a cluttered Chippendale desk. Squatting on hands and knees, he discovered that one of Rover's biscuits had been rolled into the extreme angle of the wall, and when he moved this he saw a mouse's face staring at him, with hostility it seemed, out of two beady black eyes.

"Damn it all!" said the Major violently. "Must m'dog's biscuits be pilfered under my very nose?" At this the mouse took fright and reversed, leaving a long, very long tail in view. Obeying a primeval instinct of the chase, the Major pounced on this tail and whisked the mouse, dangling, into the air. For an instant he held it in triumph, then it turned, ran up its own tail, as it were, and bit his thumb. He dropped it, and it darted under the table and out of sight.

"Perdition take it, the place is like a zoo," said the Major furiously, and he wrapped a handkerchief round his thumb. Now he began to understand why plates of food were mysteriously poised on the tops of tall vases. He went out onto the doorstep, where Rover was finishing the biscuits in a hurried manner, unbefitting to so large and dignified a hound.

When Miss Murdeigh and Miss Lambrette appeared, the Major was pacing like a caged lion.

"Ah, my dear Major Teape," said Miss Murdeigh. "May I introduce my friend Constantia Lambrette?"

The Major quailed a little as an unbelievably frail, bent, grey figure approached him, and a pair of eyes, bluer than the June sky, slowly swam up to peer at him. He was reminded of the brilliant, mysterious gaze of some rare water bird. He knew that Miss Lambrette had an international reputation; even Harpo Marx had been awed by her remarkable presence when they played together at a Victory concert.

Under that penetrating blue gaze, with the pressure of that fragile claw on his hand, the Major stammered a few words to the effect that he could not, of course, accept the Liefmehr birds without having them valued by an expert, and he suggested young George Thorless.

"Ah, yes, poor George," said Miss Murdeigh. "Ah, yes indeed, poor George. Very well, then, my dear friend, you ring him up. In that way perhaps we shall kill *several* birds with one stone. And until then we are pleased to be reunited with our feathered friends again, for a short spell."

The Major fled back to his own house, leaving the two old

creatures gazing after him like astronomers who have seen an unusual, but predicted, comet swing past.

"I will milk, dear one, while you do your practising," Miss Murdeigh said after a moment or two. "The cows do enjoy it so."

Presently, therefore, the sweet and accomplished twangling of the harp stole out into the summer dusk while the Jerseys stood flapping their thoughtful ears and drinking it in.

Meanwhile, in his garage the Major was having his daily battle with the engine that supplied his electricity. Poking about in the dim light, he first turned on the petrol, which began to drip down at a great rate and leak into a rusty cocoa tin. Then, cursing and panting, he repeatedly pulled a switch for about ten minutes until the engine, for no discernible reason, suddenly gave a hoarse asthmatic wheeze and coughed itself into riotous life. The house at once leapt out of the gloom in a torrential flood of light, every window blazing.

After waiting a moment or two to make sure that it was not going to die again at once (a frequent occurrence), the Major switched over the engine to tractor vaporising oil and stumped off indoors, where his daughter, Sally, had supper ready for him.

He looked and felt cross—heaven knew there were enough things in life to plague him, with that infernal engine which would probably drop to bits before the electric grid reached them, the state of his tenant's house, and her cockeyed notions about payment.

He strode to the telephone and dialled.

"That you, George?" he yelled. "How are you keeping? It's been a long time. I know, I know, you're busy, so are we busy, but you ought to look us up sometimes. It must be two years. No, no, far too busy to call on *you*, keeping things going here. Better when this miserable electricity comes, if it ever does. Got a job for you, George, a valuation job. Want you to come up to Orchard Cottage and look at a kind of musical box old Miss Murdeigh's offering me. Pair of birds under a glass case. But you'll have to bring some keys or bits of wire; she's lost the key, needless to say."

He listened for a moment, shouted, "Good-bye," thumped down the receiver, came over to the table, and began to drink his soup.

Damn, said Sally to herself inwardly. Damn, damn, double

damn. Oh, well, I shall fix to be out when he comes. I can be getting on with Goldenrod's portrait.

"Funny thing how George can hear quite well on the phone," the Major said, starting on his boiled eggs and cold ham, the supper he ate every day, year in, year out, "when you think he's deaf as a post to speak to. He thinks the thing might be worth quite a bit. If they did buy Orchard Cottage and we had some money in hand, we could sell the rotary scythe and put down the first payment on a cultivator. And we could get all sorts of things when the electricity comes."

He fell to brooding pleasantly over his tea.

Machinery, thought Sally. You'd think people would be wise to it by now. Spoiling your ability to do things for yourself, and then going wrong when you've come to depend on it. If it doesn't electrocute you first, or cut you in half.

She often wondered how her father managed to survive, but he seemed to bear a charmed life among his temperamental sorcerer's apprentices. Unlike George Thorless.

It was two years since George's tragedy. Sally's pity and grief for him still burned in her so painfully that her mind swung away like a shying horse from the thought of him.

George had been training as an auctioneer and valuer when the war came. He had taken to flying with enthusiasm, and became a civil air pilot when hostilities ended. He fell in love with a very beautiful girl, Dilys Heron, who became an air hostess in order to see as much of him as possible, and she was on board the ill-fated airliner that was accidentally shot down by Chinese guerrillas on its way out to Japan. Dilys was killed and George survived, with one leg and permanent total deafness.

Sally had become used to meeting George and Dilys sometimes about the lanes, and to battening down her agony of unspoken love. She had known at eighteen, and she knew now at twenty-four, that she wanted no one else in the world but George, and that she might as well hanker after Cleopatra's Needle. But what was still more unendurable was to see nowadays George's look of clenched, icy reserve and the bitter line of his mouth, shut like a trap. His deafness prevented his taking up his original job of auctioneer, and he had bought the old forge and lived on his pension, occasional odd jobs of valuation, and a bit of smithing and ornamental ironwork.

"It's a mysterious thing, you know," old Dr. Coulthurst had said to Sally once in an expansive moment, "there's no organic reason for George's deafness so far as I can discover; if I was one of those psychologists, which thank God I'm not, I'd say he was deliberately shutting himself off from humankind. He needs some sort of a shock."

Sally did her best to avoid George. Pride had kept her calm and heart-whole to all appearance in the face of George's overwhelming attachment to Dilys, and pride now helped her to live her life with courage and good sense.

Next day accordingly she took her paints and easel into the paddock where Goldenrod, the pig, lived, and began painting his portrait, which was in due course to become the new signboard for the Pig and Whistle.

It was a pleasant occupation. Goldenrod rootled and grunted; when he moved too far away Sally flung down a handful of pig-nuts to tempt him back, but he was a sociable creature and mostly stayed near at hand while she roughed in his luscious curves and the spreading Landrace ears that earned him his nickname of Dumbo in the village.

After an hour or so Goldenrod pricked the ear that was pointing towards the garden gate and Sally saw her father coming along pushing the rotary scythe. Once through the gate he stooped, puffed, swore, and pulled the starter string thirty or forty times. Letting out a roar of vindictive noise the machine then tore itself loose from him and launched off towards Goldenrod, who, thoroughly alarmed, broke away and dashed through the orchard hedge into the lane. There was a shout from the other side of the hedge, a horse's terrified whinny, a fusillade of squeals and a thudding of hoofs, all faintly to be heard above the noise of the scythe, which, with the bit between its teeth, had come up against a tree and was chattering in impotent rage.

"Turn that thing off, Sally," shouted the Major. "Someone's in trouble in the lane."

Sally approached the motor and switched it off while her father pushed through the hedge, shouting, "Are you all right?" Then there was an ominous hush, save for the sound of Goldenrod, peacefully grunting among the Queen Anne's lace.

"It's George!" the Major shouted. "He's been thrown!"

Hollow with suspense, Sally hesitated, and then peered through the hedge to see her father supporting George, who looked sick and dazed.

"Thanks," he was saying icily. "Of course it was stupid of me to ride up here on a raw colt that I'd just shod for the first time."

"But are you all right, my dear chap?" the Major shouted again anxiously. "How about the leg?"

"The good one's all right. The tin one's twisted round the wrong way."

Listening to George's tone, Sally dug her nails into her hands and prayed that her father would leave the subject. He did so.

"We'd better go up to the cottage—it's nearer than my place. I expect Miss Murdeigh will have a bit of brandy—so long as there isn't a dead mouse floating in it, ha ha! Now, how are we to manage? Sally," he yelled, "where are you? Come and take George's other arm, will you?"

"I'm all right, I can manage perfectly well like this."

The walk up to the cottage was fortunately brief.

Sally said nothing—the difficulties of communicating with George were too great. She kept her eyes averted from him. She was in terror of the scene with the two old ladies, but oddly enough their attentions did not seem to distress George.

Miss Murdeigh quietly sat him down, looked at his knee, put a cold compress on it, and said it would be all right in a few minutes. She did not fuss or exclaim, and George seemed strangely at ease looking round him at the unbelievable clutter, with the bitter lines for once smoothed from his face.

Miss Lambrette had tottered off and now reappeared with a crystal decanter, very dusty.

"No brandy, I am afraid," Miss Murdeigh said. "But perhaps a little Tio Pepe—?"

"I oughtn't to," the Major said longingly when it was offered him. "With my liver . . . but I can't resist it."

Sally sipped her sherry quietly, listening to the muted flutter of the swallows that were nesting under the mantelpiece and watching from the corner of her eye a golden reflection dance from his drink onto George's lean jaw. How peaceful it would be, she mused, if George and I were paying a morning call on the old ladies, and afterwards we'd stroll back to the forge and he'd clink and clank on the anvil or grind away at the bellows while I cut bread and cheese and drew a jugful of cider.

She shut her eyes, seduced by this fancy, but opened them again when she heard George's hesitant voice.

"Is that the piece you wanted me to see? Perhaps I could be having a look at it."

Sally suppressed a smile at her first sight of the birds, but George took them seriously enough. He removed the glass case, turned the whole contraption upside down, and studied it carefully. Then he brought out from his pocket various keys and bits of wire and began trying them in the little keyhole.

"It's a Liefmehr, without a doubt," he said politely to Miss Murdeigh, who was watching him with a lock of grey hair falling over her bright eyes. "Do you know its history?"

"It was given me by the Duke of Medina Sidonia," she told him. "Of its history before it came into his possession I know nothing."

"Speak up," the Major muttered. "Don't forget the feller's deaf."

"It's supposed to have an unusual gift," Miss Murdeigh went on in a piercing voice, "that of granting a wish to any person hearing it for the first time."

"Bosh," grunted the Major to himself, and he said sceptically, "Has it ever granted a wish for you, Miss Murdeigh?"

Miss Murdeigh shook her head. "But then I have never played it," she added. "I lost the key in Madrid. And then, you know, I am so contented that I really have nothing left to wish for."

"Ah," said George suddenly. A click sounded from the interior of the mechanism. He began winding with a piece of bent wire, turning it carefully and slowly. His glance just brushed Sally, silent in her corner, and then all at once he smiled. I haven't seen *that* smile for five years, Sally thought. It was like unexpectedly meeting an old friend in the streets of a foreign city. She found that she was holding on tightly to the arms of her chair.

"You should all shut your eyes," Miss Murdeigh commanded. Obediently they did so.

Oh, thought Sally, all her mind, her being, clenched on the one object. Make him better, make him better.

Dilys. George's mind went on its accustomed track. If only I could forgive myself for letting you come. If only I could be sure you hadn't suffered.

Unaware that he did so, he moved his head like someone trying to avoid unbearable pain.

That damned electric light, grumbled the Major to himself. Bound to come some year, I suppose.

The old ladies' eyes met, smiling across the birds as George's fingers finished their winding. Miss Murdeigh looked round the littered room contentedly, and she pushed a crumb of cheese nearer to a confiding mouse who was sitting at her elbow.

Then the birds began their dance. It was the sound of the music, so astonishingly like laughter, that first penetrated George's darkness. He couldn't help it; he opened his eyes. And then kept them open, watching with incredulous pleasure the extraordinary galvanic hopping jig the birds were performing.

Sally heard the ludicrous sweet piping, and then she heard George laugh. She opened her eyes and saw him throw himself back in his chair, helpless and crowing with mirth, wiping the tears from his eyes. They were all laughing; Sally's ribs seemed to have ached all her life and she thought she would never breathe again; frail Miss Lambrette gave vent to an astonishing sonorous guffaw; even the upright Major was choking and mopping his eyes. There was something perfectly irresistible about the innocent, sugary tune accompanying that frantic flapping dance.

Oh, don't let it stop, don't let it ever stop, Sally thought, but already the birds were slowing down, and one of them suddenly flung itself forward in a last frenzied effort, right off its perch and onto the floor, while the other fell backward in an attitude of drunken exhaustion, and with a grinding jerk the music came to an end.

"By Jove," said the Major. "Don't know when I've laughed like that. Comical little beggars. But I'm afraid it's done it no good to play it, Miss Murdeigh."

"Alas, I fear it was their swansong," Miss Murdeigh agreed philosophicaly. "Has the mainspring gone, Mr. Thorless?"

He nodded. "I'm sorry. I very much doubt if it can be repaired now—it's just shaken itself to bits."

"And so we shall have, after all, to continue paying you rent," said Miss Murdeigh to the Major, but she did not seem dismayed at the prospect. Indeed, Sally thought, there was a glint of amusement in her eye.

"Maybe it's as well." The Major grunted heavily. "Roof would be like a sieve and you'd probably be living in two foot of water without noticing it if I didn't give you a once-over from time to time."

"Well I must be going back," Sally murmured, "I left some lentils in the oven." Then she suddenly stood still. "*George!*"

He looked at her, smiling.

"You heard what Miss Murdeigh said! About the mainspring! And she wasn't shouting."

"I suppose I did," he agreed.

"You're hearing me!" He nodded again, looking a little shamefaced this time.

"Oh, you are irritating!" exclaimed Sally. Violently, inexplicably, she burst into tears and ran from the room. Wordlessly answering Miss Murdeigh's raised eybrow, George limped rapidly after her.

"Well," muttered the Major, "I suppose it was that fall that did it. Most remarkable thing, most. I say, though, Miss Murdeigh, are you sure you wouldn't like Orchard Cottage as a gift? It seems such a damned shame about those birds being broken."

Miss Murdeigh gave him her sweet, inscrutable smile. "Really, do you know, I'd sooner go on paying you rent."

" 'Fraid I haven't always been a very good neighbour," the Major went on awkwardly. "But I tell you what, as soon as the electricity comes along I'm going to sell Goldenrod and get a TV set, and then you must come up and watch whenever you like."

He stumped off home, to the long blue envelope that awaited him with its undreamed-of mechanical possibilities.

Miss Murdeigh and Miss Lambrette fed the mice and sat down comfortably to play a sonata by Pousset.

The Man Who Had Seen the Rope Trick

"Miss Drake," said Mrs. Minser. "When ye've finished with the salt and pepper, will ye please put them *together*?"

"Sorry, I'm sorry," mumbled Miss Drake. "I can't see very well as you know, I can't see very well." Her tremulous hands worked out like tendrils across the table and succeeded in knocking the mustard onto its side. An ochre blob defiled the snowy stiffness of the tablecloth. Mrs. Minser let a slight hiss escape her.

"That's the *third* tablecloth ye've dirtied in a week, Miss Drake. Do ye know I had to get up at four o'clock this morning to do all the washing? I shann't be able to keep ye if ye go on like this, ye know."

Without waiting for the whispered apologies she turned towards the dining-room door, pushing the trolley with the meat plates before her. Her straw-grey hair was swept to a knot on the top of her head, her grey eyes were as opaque as bottle tops, her mouth was screwed tight shut against the culpabilities of other people.

"Stoopid business, gettin' up at four in the mornin'," muttered old Mr. Hill, but he muttered it quietly to himself. "Who cares about a blob of mustard on the tablecloth, anyway? Who cares about a tablecloth, or a separate table, if the food's good? If she's got to get up at four, why don't she make us some decent porridge instead of the slime she gives us?"

He bowed his head prayerfully over his bread plate as Mrs. Minser returned, weaving her way with the neatness of long practice between the white-covered tables, each with its silent, elderly, ruminating diner.

The food was *not* good. "Rice shape or banana, Mr. Hill?" Mrs Minser asked, pausing beside him.

"Banana, thank'ee." He repressed a shudder as he looked at the colourless, glutinous pudding. The bananas were unripe, and bad for his indigestion, but at least they were palatable.

"Mr. Wakefield! Ye've spotted yer shirt with gravy! That means more washing, and I've got a new guest coming tomorrow. I cann't think how you old people can be so inconsiderate."

"I'll wash it, I'll wash it myself, Mrs. Minser." The old man put an anxious, protective hand over the spot.

"Ye'll do no such thing!"

"Who is the new guest then, Mrs. Minser?" Mr. Hill asked, more to distract her attention from his neighbour's misfortune than because he wanted to know.

"A Mr. Ollendod. Retired from India. I only hope," said Mrs. Minser forebodingly, "that he won't have a great deal of luggage, else where we shall put it all I cann't imagine."

"India," murmured Mr. Hill to himself. "From India, eh? He'll certainly find it different here." And he looked round the dining room of the Balmoral Guest House. The name Balmoral, and Mrs. Minser's lowland accent, constituted the only Scottish elements in the guest house, which was otherwise pure Westcliff. The sea, half a mile away, invisible from the house, was implicit in the bracingness of the air and the presence of so many elderly residents pottering out twice a day to listen to the municipal orchestra. Nobody actually swam in the sea, or even looked at it much, but there it was anyway, a guarantee of ozone and fresh fish on the tables of the residential hotels.

Mr. Ollendod arrived punctually next day, and he did have a lot of luggage.

Mrs. Minser's expression became more and more ominous as trunks and cases—some of them very foreign-looking and made of straw—boxes and rolls and bundles were unloaded.

"Where does he think all that is going?" she said incautiously loudly to her husband, who was helping to carry in the cases.

Mr. Ollendod was an elderly, very brown, shrivelled little man, but he evidently had all his faculties intact, for he looked up from paying the cab driver to say, "In my room, I trust, naturally. It is a double room, is it not? Did I not stipulate for a double room?"

Mrs. Minser's idea of a double room was one into which a double bed could be squeezed. She eyed Mr. Ollendod measuringly, her lips pursed together. Was he going to be the sort who gave trouble? If so, she'd soon find a reason for giving him his notice. Summer was coming, when prices and the demand for rooms went up; one could afford to be choosy. Still, ten guineas a week was ten guineas; it would do no harm to wait and see.

The Minser children, Martin and Jenny, came home from school and halted, fascinated, amongst Mr. Ollendod's possessions.

"Look, a screen, all covered with pictures!"

"He's got spears!"

"A tigerskin!"

"An elephant's foot!"

"What's this, a shield?"

"No, it's a fan, made of peacocks' feathers." Mr. Ollendod smiled at them benevolently. Jenny thought that his face looked like the skin on top of cocoa, wrinkling when you stir it.

"Is he an Indian, mother?" she asked when they were in the kitchen.

"No, of course he's not. He's just brown because he's lived in a hot climate," Mrs. Minser said sharply. "Run and do yer homework and stay out from under my feet."

The residents also were discussing Mr. Ollendod.

"Do you think he can be—*foreign?*" whispered Mrs. Pursey. "He is such an odd-looking man. His eyes are so bright—just like diamonds. What do you think, Miss Drake?"

"How should I know?" snapped Miss Drake. "You seem to forget I haven't been able to see across the room for the last five years."

The children soon found their way to Mr. Ollendod's room. They were strictly forbidden to speak to or mix with the guests in any way, but there was an irresistible attraction about the little bright-eyed man and his belongings.

"Tell us about India," Jenny said, stroking the snarling tiger's head with its great yellow glass eyes.

"India? The hills are blue and wooded, they look as innocent as Essex but they're full of tigers and snakes and swinging, chattering monkeys. In the villages you can smell dust and dung smoke and incense; there are no brown or grey clothes, but flashing pinks and blood reds, turquoises and saffrons; the cows have horns three yards wide."

"Shall you ever go back there?" Martin asked, wondering how anybody could bear to exchange such a place for the worn grey, black, and fawn carpeting, the veneer wardrobe and plate glass, the limp yellow sateen coverlid of a Balmoral bedroom.

"No," said Mr. Olendod, sighing. "I fell ill. And no one wants me there now. Still," he added more cheerfully, "I have brought back plenty of reminders with me, enough to keep India alive in my mind. Look at this—and this—and this."

Everything was wonderful—the curved leather slippers, the richly patterned silk of Mr. Ollendod's dressing gown and scarves, the screen with its exotic pictures ("I'm not letting *that* stay there long," said Mrs. Minser), the huge pink shells with a sheen of pearl, the gnarled and grinning images, the hard, scented sweets covered with coloured sugar.

"You are *not* to go up there. And if he offers you anything to eat, you are to throw it straight away," Mrs. Minser said, but she might as well have spoken to the wind. The instant the children had done their homework they were up in Mr. Ollendod's room, demanding stories of snakes and werewolves, of crocodiles who lived for a hundred years, of mysterious ceremonies in temples, ghosts who walked with their feet swivelled backwards on their ankles, and women with the evil eye who could turn milk sour and rot the unripe fruit on a neighbour's vine.

"You've really seen it? You've seen them? You've seen a snake charmer and a snake standing on its tail? And a lizard break in half and each half run away separately? And an eagle fly away with a live sheep?"

"All those things," he said. "I'll play you a snake charmer's tune if you like."

He fished a little bamboo flageolet out of a cedarwood box and began to play a tune that consisted of no more than a few trickling, monotonous notes, repeated over and over again. Tuffy, the aged, moth-eaten black cat who followed the children everywhere when they were at home and dozed in Mr. Ollendod's armchair when they were at school, woke up, and pricked up his ears; downstairs, Jip, the bad-tempered Airedale, growled gently in his throat; and Mrs. Minser, sprinkling water on her starched ironing, paused and angrily rubbed her ear as if a mosquito had tickled it.

"And I've seen another thing: a rope that stands on its tail when the man says a secret word to it, stands straight up on end! And a boy climbs up it, right up! Higher and higher, till he finally disappears out of sight."

"Where does he go to?" the children asked, huge-eyed.

"A country where the grass grows soft and patterned like a carpet, where the deer wear gold necklets and come to your hand for pieces of bread, where the plums are red and sweet and as big as oranges, and the girls have voices like singing birds."

"Does he never come back?"

"Sometimes he jumps down out of the sky with his hands full of wonderful grass and fruits. But sometimes he never comes back."

"Do *you* know the word they say to the rope?"

"I've heard it, yes."

"If I were the boy I wouldn't come back," said Jenny. "Tell us some more. About the witch woman who fans herself."

"She fans herself with a peacock-feather fan," Mr. Ollendod said. "And when she does that she becomes a snake and slips away into the forest. And when she is tired of being a snake and wants to turn into a woman again, she taps her husband's foot with her cold head till he waves the fan over her."

"Is the fan just like yours on the wall?"

"Just like it."

"Oh, may we fan ourselves with it, may we?"

"And turn yourselves into little snakes? What would your mother say?" asked Mr. Ollendod, laughing heartily.

Mrs. Minser had plenty to say as it was. When the children told her a garbled mixture of the snakes and the deer and the live rope and girls with birds' voices and plums as big as oranges, she pursed her lips together tight.

"A pack of moonshine and rubbish! I've a good mind to forbid him to speak to them."

"Oh, come, Hannah," her husband said mildly. "He keeps them out of mischief for hours on end. You know you can't stand it if they come into the kitchen or make a noise in the garden. And he's only telling them Indian fairy tales."

"Well anyway ye're not to believe a word he says," Mrs. Minser ordered the children. "Not a *single* word."

She might as well have spoken to the wind. . . .

Tuffy, the cat, fell ill and lay with faintly heaving sides in the middle of the hallway. Mrs. Minser exclaimed angrily when she found Mr. Ollendod bending over him.

"That dirty old cat! It's high time he was put away."

"It is a cold he has, nothing more," Mr. Ollendod said mildly. "If you will allow me, I shall take him to my room and treat him. I have some Indian gum which is very good for inhaling."

But Mrs. Minser refused to consider the idea. She rang up the vet, and when the children came home from school, Tuffy was gone.

They found their way up to Mr. Ollendod's room, speechless with grief.

He looked at them thoughtfully for a while and then said, "Shall I tell you a secret?"

"Yes, what? What?" Martin said, and Jenny cried, "You've got Tuffy hidden here, is that it?"

"Not exactly," said Mr. Ollendod, "but you see that mirror on the wall?"

"The big one covered with a fringy shawl, yes?"

"Once upon a time that mirror belonged to a queen in India. She was very beautiful, so beautiful that it was said sick people could be cured of their illnesses just by looking at her. In course of time she grew old and lost her beauty. But the mirror remembered how beautiful she had been and showed her still the lovely face she had lost. And one day she walked right into the mirror and was never seen again. So if you look into it, you do not see things as they are now, but beautiful as they were in their youth."

"May we look?"

"Just for a short time you may. Climb on the chair," Mr. Ollendod said, smiling, and they climbed up and peered into the mirror, while he steadied them with a hand on each of their necks.

"Oh!" cried Jenny, "I can see him; I can see Tuffy! He's a kitten again, chasing grasshoppers."

"I can see him too!" shouted Martin, jumping up and down. The chair overbalanced and tipped them onto the floor.

"Let us look again, please let us!"

"Not today," said Mr. Ollendod. "If you look too long into that mirror, you, like the queen, might vanish into it for good. That is why I keep it covered with a shawl."

The children went away comforted, thinking of Tuffy young and frolicsome once more, chasing butterflies in the sun. Mr. Ollendod gave them a little ivory chess set, to distract them from missing their cat, but Mrs. Minser, saying it was too good for children and that they would only spoil it, sold it and put the money in the post office "for later on."

It was July now. The weather grew daily warmer and closer. Mrs. Minser told Mr. Ollendod that she was obliged to raise his rent by three guineas "for the summer prices." She rather hoped this would make him leave, but he paid up.

"I'm old and tired," he said. "I don't want to move again, for I may not be here very long. One of these days my heart will carry me off."

And, in fact, one oppressive, thundery day he had a bad heart attack and had to stay in bed for a week.

"I certainly don't want him if he's going to be ill all the time," Mrs. Minser said to her husband. "I shall tell him that we want his room as soon as he's better." In the meantime she put away as many as possible of the Indian things, saying that they were a dust-collecting nuisance in the sickroom. She left the swords and the fan and the mirror, because they hung on the wall, out of harm's way.

As she had promised, the minute Mr. Ollendod was up and walking around again, she told him his room was wanted and he must go.

"But where?" he said, standing so still, leaning on his stick, that Mrs. Minser had the uneasy notion for a moment that the clock on the wall had stopped ticking to listen for her answer.

"That's no concern of mine," she said coldly. "Go where you please, wherever anyone can be found who'll take you with all this rubbish."

"I must think this over," said Mr. Ollendod. He put on his Panama hat and walked slowly down to the beach. The tide was out, revealing a mile of flat, pallid mud studded with baked-bean tins. Jenny and Martin were there, listlessly trying to fly a homemade kite. Not a breath of wind stirred and the kite kept flopping down in the mud, but they knew that if they went home before six their mother would send them out again.

"There's Mr. Ollendod," said Jenny.

"Perhaps he could fly the kite," said Martin.

They ran to him, leaving two black parallel trails in the shining goo.

"Mr. Ollendod, can you fly our kite?"

"It needs someone to run with it *very* fast."

He smiled at them kindly. Even the slowest stroll now made his heart begin to race and stumble.

"Let's see," he said. He held the string for a moment in his hands and was silent; then he said, "I can't run with it, but perhaps I can persuade it to go up of its own accord."

The children watched, silent and attentive, while he murmured something to the rope in a low voice that they could not quite catch.

"Look, it's moving," whispered Martin.

The kite, which had been hanging limp, suddenly twitched and jerked like a fish at the end of a line, then, by slow degrees, drew itself up and, as if invisibly pulled from above, began to climb higher and higher into the warm grey sky. Mr. Ollendod kept his eyes fixed on it; Jenny noticed that his hands were clenched and the sweat was rolling off his forehead.

"It's like the story!" exclaimed Martin. "The man with the rope and the magic word and the boy who climbs it—may we climb it? We've learnt how to at school."

Mr. Ollendod couldn't speak, but they took his silence as consent. They flung themselves at the rope and swarmed up it. Mr. Ollendod, still holding onto the end of the rope, gradually lowered himself to the ground and sat with his head bowed over his knees; then with a slow subsiding motion he fell over onto his side. His hands relaxed on the rope, which swung softly upwards and disappeared; after a while the tide came in and washed away three sets of footprints.

"Those children are very late," said Mrs. Minser at six o'clock. "Are they up in Mr. Ollendod's room?"

She went up to see. The room was empty.

"I shall let it to a couple, next time," reflected Mrs. Minser, picking up the peacock-feather fan and fanning herself, for the heat was oppressive. "A couple will pay twice the rent and they are more likely to eat meals out. I wonder where those children can have got to? . . ."

An hour later old Mr. Hill, on his way down to supper, looked through Mr. Ollendod's open door and saw a snake wriggling about on the carpet. He called out excitedly. By the time Mr. Minser had come up, the snake had slid under the bed and Mrs. Pursey was screaming vigorously. Mr. Minser rattled a stick and the snake shot out towards his foot, but he was ready with a sharp scimitar snatched from the wall, and cut off its head. The old people, clustered in a dithering group outside the door, applauded his quickness.

"Fancy Mr. Ollendod's keeping a pet snake all this time and we never knew!" shuddered Mrs. Pursey. "I hope he hasn't anything else of the kind in here." Inquisitively she ventured in. "Why, what a beautiful mirror!" she cried. The others followed, pushing and chattering, looking about greedily.

Mr. Minser brushed through the group irritably and went downstairs with the decapitated snake. "I shall sound the gong for supper in five minutes," he called. "Hannah, Hannah! Where are you? Nothing's going as it should in this house today."

But Hannah, needless to say, did not reply, and when he banged the gong in five minutes, nobody came down but blind old Miss Drake, who said rather peevishly that all the others had slipped away and left her behind in Mr. Ollendod's room.

"Slipped away! And left me! Among all his horrid things! Without saying a word, so inconsiderate! Anything might have happened to me."

And she started quickly eating up Mrs. Pursey's buttered toast.

The Cold Flame

I WAS asleep when Patrick rang up. The bell sliced through a dream about this extraordinary jampot factory, a kind of rose-red brick catacomb, much older than time, sunk deep on top of the Downs, and I was not pleased to be woken. I groped with a blind arm and worked the receiver in between my ear and the pillow.

"Ellis? Is that you?"

"Of course it is," I snarled. "Who else do you expect in my bed at three a.m.? Why in heaven's name ring up at this time?"

"I'm sorry," he said, sounding muffled and distant and apologetic. "Where I am it's only half-past something." A sort of oceanic roar separated us for a moment, then I heard him say, ". . . rang you as soon as I could."

"Well, where are you?"

Then I woke up a bit more and interrupted as he began speaking again. "Hey, I thought you were supposed to be dead! There were headlines in the evening papers—a climbing accident. Was it a mistake then?"

"No, I'm dead right enough. I fell into the crater of a volcano."

"What were you doing on a *volcano*, for goodness' sake?"

"Lying on the lip writing a poem about what it looked like inside. The bit I was lying on broke off." Patrick sounded regretful. "It would have been a good poem too."

Patrick was a poet, perhaps I should explain. Had been a poet. Or said he was. No one had ever seen his poetry because he steadfastly refused to let anybody read his work, though he insisted, with a quiet self-confidence not otherwise habitual to him, that the poems were very good indeed. In no other respect was he remarkable, but most people quite liked Patrick; he was a lanky, amusing creature with guileless blue eyes and a passion for singing sad, randy songs when he had had a drink or two. For some time I had been a little in love with Patrick. I was sorry to hear he was dead.

"Look, Patrick," I began again. "Are you sure you're dead?"

"Of course I'm sure."

"Where are you then?"

"Lord knows. I've hardly had time to look round yet. There's something on my mind; that's why I contacted you."

The word contacted seemed inappropriate. I said, "Why ring up?"

"I could appear if you'd prefer it."

Remembering the cause of his death, I said hastily, "No, no, let's go on as we are. What's on your mind?"

"It's my poems, Ellis. Could you get them published, do you think?"

My heart sank a bit, as anybody's does at this sort of request from a friend, but I said, "Where are they?"

"At my flat. A big thick stack of quarto paper, all handwritten. In my desk."

"Okay. I'll see what I can do. But listen, love—I don't want to sound a gloomy note, but suppose no publisher will touch them—what then? Promise you won't hold me responsible? Keep hanging around, you know, haunting, that kind of thing?"

"No, of course not," he said quickly. "But you needn't worry. Those poems are good. There's a picture at the flat as well, though, behind the wardrobe, with its face to the wall. As a matter of fact, it's a portrait of my mother. It's by Chapedelaine—done before he made his name. About seven years ago I got him to paint her for her birthday present (this was before I quarrelled with Mother, of course). But she didn't like it—said it was hideous—so I gave her a bottle of scent instead. Now, of course, it's worth a packet. You can get Sowerby's to auction it, and the proceeds would certainly pay for the publication of the poems, if necessary.

But only in the last resort, mind you! I'm convinced those poems can stand on their own. I'm only sorry I didn't finish the volcano one—maybe I could dictate it—"

"I really must get some sleep," I broke in, thinking what a good thing it was they hadn't got direct dialing yet between this world and the next. "I'll go round to your flat first thing tomorrow. I've still got the key. Good-bye, Patrick."

And I clonked back the receiver on its rest and tried to return to my lovely deep-hidden jampot factory among the brooding Downs. Gone beyond recall.

Next day at Patrick's flat I found I had been forestalled. The caretaker told me that a lady, Mrs. O'Shea, had already called there and taken away all her son's effects.

I was wondering how to inform Patrick of this development—he hadn't left a number—when he got through to me again on his own phone. At the news I had to relate he let out a cry of anguish.

"Not Mother! God, what'll we do now? Ellis, that woman's a vulture. You'll have the devil's own job prising the poems out of her."

"Why not just get in touch with her direct—the way you did with me—and tell *her* to send the poems to a publisher?" I said. "Suggest trying Chatto first."

"You don't understand! For one thing, I couldn't get near her. For another, she has this grudge against me; when I gave up going home it really dealt her a mortal blow. It'd give her the most exquisite pleasure to thwart me. No, I'm afraid you'll have to use all your tact and diplomacy, Ellis; you'd better drive down to Clayhole tomorrow—"

"But look here! Supposing she won't—"

No answer. Patrick had disconnected.

So next afternoon found me driving down to Clayhole. I had never been to Patrick's home—nor had Patrick since the quarrel with his mother. I was quite curious to see her, as a matter of fact; Patrick's discriptions of her had been so conflicting. Before the breach she was the most wonderful mother in the world, fun, pretty, sympathetic, witty—while after it, no language had been too virulent to describe her, a sort of female Dracula, tyrannical, humourless, blood-sucking.

One thing I did notice as I approached the house—up a steep, stony, unmetalled lane—the weather had turned a bit colder. The leaves hung on the trees like torn rags, the ground was hard as iron, the sky leaden.

Mrs. O'Shea received me with the utmost graciousness. But in spite of this I retained a powerful impression that I had arrived at an awkward moment; perhaps she had been about to bathe the dog, or watch a favourite programme, or start preparing a meal. She was a small, pretty Irishwoman her curling hair a beautiful white, her skin a lovely tea-rose pink, her eyes the curious opaque blue that goes with real granite obstinacy. One odd feature of her face was that she appeared to have no lips; they were so pale they disappeared into her powdered cheeks. I could see why Patrick had never mentioned his father. Major O'Shea stood beside his wife, but he was a nonentity: a stooped, watery-eyed, dangling fellow, whose only function was to echo his wife's opinions.

The house was a pleasant Queen Anne manor, furnished in excellent taste with chintz and Chippendale, and achingly, freezingly cold. I had to clench my teeth to stop them chattering. Mrs. O'Shea, in her cashmere twinset and pearls, seemed impervious to the glacial temperature, but the Major's cheeks were blue; every now and then a drop formed at the tip of his nose which he carefully wiped away with a spotless silk handkerchief. I began to understand why Patrick had been keen on volcanoes.

They stood facing me like an interview board while I explained my errand. I began by saying how grieved I had been to hear of Patrick's death, and spoke of his lovable nature and unusual promise. The Major did look genuinely grieved, but Mrs. O'Shea was smiling, and there was something about her smile that irritated me profoundly.

I then went on to say that I had received a communication from Patrick since his death, and waited for reactions. They were sparse. Mrs. O'Shea's lips tightened fractionally, the Major's lids dropped over his lugubrious milky tea-coloured eyes; that was all.

"You don't seem surprised," I said cautiously. "You were expecting something of the kind perhaps?"

"No, not particularly," Mrs. O'Shea said. She sat down, placed her feet on a footstool, and picked up a circular embroidery frame. "My family is psychic, however; this kind of thing is not unusual. What did Patrick want to say?"

"It was about his poems."

"Oh, yes?" Her tone was as colourless as surgical spirit. She carefully chose a length of silk. Her glance flickered once to the object she was using as a footstool: a solid pile of papers about a foot thick, wrapped up clumsily in an old grey cardigan which looked as if it had once lined a dog basket; it was matted with white terrier hairs.

My heart sank.

"I believe you have his poems now? Patrick is most anxious that they should be published."

"And I'm not at all anxious they should be published," Mrs. O'Shea said with her most irritating smile.

"Quite, quite," the Major assented.

We argued about it. Mrs. O'Shea had three lines of argument: first, that no one in her family had ever written poetry, therefore Patrick's poems were sure to be hopeless; second, that no one in her family had ever written poetry and, even in the totally unlikely event of the poems being any good, it was a most disreputable thing to do; third, that Patrick was conceited, ungrateful, and self-centred, and it would do him nothing but harm to see his poems in print. She spoke as if he were still alive.

"Besides," she added, "I'm sure no publisher would look at them."

"You have read them?"

"Heavens, no!" She laughed. "I've no time for such rubbish."

"But if a publisher did take them?"

"You'd never get one to risk his money on such a venture."

I explained Patrick's plans regarding the Chapdelaine portrait. The O'Sheas looked sceptical. "You perhaps have it here?" I asked.

"A hideous thing. Nobody in their senses would give enough money for that to get a book published."

"I'd very much like to see it, all the same."

"Roderick, take Miss Bell to look at the picture," Mrs. O'Shea said, withdrawing another strand of silk.

The picture was in the attic, face down. I saw at once why Mrs. O'Shea had not liked it. Chapdelaine had done a merciless job of work. It was brilliant—one of the best examples of his early Gold Period. I imagined it would fetch even more than Patrick hoped. When I explained this to the Major, an acquisitive gleam came into his eye.

"Surely that would more than pay for the publication of the poems?"

"Oh, certainly," I assured him.

"I'll see what my wife has to say."

Mrs. O'Shea was not interested in cash. She had a new line of defence. "Of course you've no actual proof that you come from Patrick, have you? I don't really see why we should take your word in the matter."

Suddenly I was furious. My rage and the deadly cold were simultaneously too much for me. I said, as politely as I could, "Since I can see you are completely opposed to my performing this small service for your son, I won't waste any more of our time," and left them abruptly. The Major looked a little taken aback, but his wife calmly pursued her stitchery.

It was good to get out of that icy, lavender-scented morgue into the fresh, windy night.

My car limped down the lane pulling to the left, but I was so angry that I had reached the village before I realised I had a flat tyre. I got out and surveyed it. The car was slumped down on one haunch as if Mrs. O'Shea had put a curse on it.

I went into the pub for a hot toddy before changing the wheel, and while I was in there the landlord said, "Would you be Miss Bell? There's a phone call for you."

It was Patrick. I told him about my failure and he cursed, but he did not seem surprised.

"Why does your mother hate you so, Patrick?"

"Because I got away from her. That's why she can't stand my poetry—because it's nothing to do with her. Anyway she can hardly read. If my father so much as picks up a book, she gets it away from him as soon as she can and hides it. Well, you can see what he's like. Sucked dry. She likes to feel she knows the whole contents of a person's mind, and that it's entirely focused on *her*. She's afraid of being left alone; she's never slept by herself in a room in her life. If ever he had to go away, she'd have my bed put in her room."

I thought about that.

"But as to your authority to act for me," Patrick went on, "we can easily fix that. Have a double whisky and get a pen and paper. Shut your eyes."

Reluctantly I complied. It was an odd sensation. I felt Patrick's light, chill clutch on my wrist, moving my hand. For a moment, the contrast with the last time I had held his hand made a strangling weight of tears rise in my throat; then I remembered Mrs. O'Shea's icy determination and realised that Patrick resembled her in this; suddenly I felt free of him, free of sorrow.

When I opened my eyes again, there was a message in Patrick's odd, angular script, to the effect that he authorised me to sell his Chapdelaine picture and use the proceeds to pay for the publication of his poems, if necessary.

The drinks had fortified me, so I got a garage to change my wheel and walked back up the lane to Clayhole. The O'Sheas had just finished their supper. They invited me civilly, but without enthusiasm, to drink coffee with them. The coffee was surprisingly good, but stone cold, served in little gold-rimmed cups the size of walnut shells. Over it Mrs. O'Shea scanned Patrick's message. I glanced round—we were in the arctic dining room—and noticed that Chapdelaine's picture had now been hung on the wall. It smiled at me with Mrs. O'Shea's own bland hostility.

"I see; very well," she said at last. "I suppose you must take the picture then."

"And the poems too, I hope."

"Oh, no. Not yet," she said. "*When* you've sold the picture, for this large sum you say it will fetch, *then* I'll see about letting you have the poems."

"But that's not—" I began, and then stopped. What was the use? She was not a logical woman, no good reasoning with her. One step at a time was as fast as one could go.

The sale of an early Chapdelaine portrait made quite a stir, and the bidding at Sowerby's began briskly. The picture was exhibited on an easel on the auctioneer's dais. From my seat in the front row I was dismayed to notice, as the bids rose past the four-figure mark, that the portrait was beginning to fade. The background remained, but by the time twenty-five hundred had been reached, Mrs. O'Shea had vanished completely. The bidding faltered and came to a stop; there were complaints. The auctioneer inspected the portrait, directed an accusing stare at me, and declared the sale null. I had to take the canvas ignominiously back to my flat, and the evening papers had humorous headlines: WHERE DID THE COLOURS RUN TO? NO BIDS FOR CHAPDELAINE'S WHITE PERIOD.

When the telephone rang, I expected that it would be Patrick and picked up the receiver gloomily, but it was a French voice.

"Armand Chapdelaine here. Miss Bell?"

"Speaking."

"We met, I think, once, a few years ago, in the company of young Patrick O'Shea. I am ringing from Paris about this odd incident of his mother's portrait."

"Oh, yes?"

"May I come and inspect the canvas, Miss Bell?"

"Of course," I said, slightly startled. "Not that there's anything to see."

"That is so kind of you. Till tomorrow, then."

Chapdelaine was a French Canadian: stocky, dark, and full of *loup-garou* charm.

After carefully scrutinising the canvas, he listened with intense interest to the tale about Patrick and his mother.

"Aha! This is a genuine piece of necromancy," he said, rubbing his hands. "I always knew there was something unusually powerful about that woman's character. She had a most profound dislike for me; I recall it well."

"Because you were her son's friend."

"Of course." He inspected the canvas again and said, "I shall be delighted to buy this from you for two thousand five hundred pounds, Miss Bell. It is the only one of my pictures that has been subjected to black magic, up to now."

"Are you quite sure?"

"Entirely sure." He gave me his engagingly wolfish smile. "Then we will see what shot Madame Mère fetches out of her locker."

Mrs. O'Shea was plainly enjoying the combat over Patrick's poems. It had given her a new interest. When she heard the news that two thousand five hundred pounds were lodged in a trust account, ready to pay for the publication of the poems, if necessary, her reaction was almost predictable.

"But that wouldn't be honest!" she said. "I suppose Mr. Chapdelaine bought the canvas out of kindness, but it can't be counted as a proper sale. The money must be returned to him." Her face set like epoxy, and she rearranged her feet more firmly on the footstool.

"On no account will I have it back, madame," Chapdelaine riposted. He had come down with me to help persuade her; he said he was dying to see her again.

"If you won't, then it must be given to charity. I'm afraid it's out of the question that I should allow money which was obtained by what amounts to false pretences to be used to promote that poor silly boy's scribblings."

"Quite, quite," said the Major.

"But it may not be necessary—" I began in exasperation. An opaque blue gleam showed for an instant in Mrs. O'Shea's eye. Chapdelaine raised a hand soothingly and I subsided. I'd known, of course, that I too was an object of her dislike, but I had not realised how very deep it went; the absolute hatred in her glance was a slight shock. It struck me that, unreasonably enough, this hate had been augmented by the fact that Chapdelaine and I were getting on rather well together.

"Since madame does not approve of our plan, I have another proposition," said Chapdelaine, who seemed to be taking a pleasure in the duel almost equal to that of Mrs. O'Shea. I felt slightly excluded. "May I be allowed to do a second portrait, and two thousand five hundred shall be the sitter's fee?"

"Humph," said Mrs. O'Shea. "I'd no great opinion of the last one ye did."

"Hideous thing. Hideous," said the Major.

"Oh, but this one, madame, will be quite different!" Chapdelaine smiled, at his most persuasive. "In the course of seven years, after all, one's technique alters entirely."

She demurred for a long time, but in the end, I suppose, she could not resist this chance of further entertainment. Besides, he was extremely well known now.

"You'll have to come down here though, Mr. Chapdelaine; at my age I can't be gadding up to London for sittings."

"Of course," he agreed, shivering slightly; the sitting room was as cold as ever. "It will be a great pleasure."

"I think the pub in the village occasionally puts up visitors," Mrs. O'Shea added. "I'll speak to them." Chapdelaine shuddered again. "But they only have one bedroom, so I'm afraid there won't be room for *you*, Miss Bell." Her tone expressed volumes.

"Thank you, but I have my job in London," I said coldly. "Besides, I'd like to be getting on with offering Patrick's poems; may I take them now, Mrs. O'Shea?"

"The?— Oh, gracious, *no*—not till the picture's finished! After all," she said with a smile of pure, chill malice, "I may not like it when it's done, may I?"

"It's a hopeless affair, hopeless!" I raged as soon as we were away from the house. "She'll always find some way of slipping out of the bargain; she's utterly unscrupulous. The woman's a fiend! Really I can't think how Patrick could ever have been fond of her. Why do you bother to go on with this?"

"Oh, but I am looking forward to painting this portrait immensely!" Chapdelaine wore a broad grin. "I feel convinced this will be the best piece of work I ever did. I shall have to get that house warmed up though, even if it means myself paying for a truckload of logs; one cannot work inside of a deep freeze."

Somehow he achieved this; when I took down a photographer to get a story, with pictures, for the magazine on which I work, we found the sitting room transformed, littered with artists' equipment and heated to conservatory temperature by a huge roaring fire. Mrs. O'Shea, evidently making the most of such unaccustomed sybaritism, was seated close by the fire, her feet, as ever, firmly planted on the blanket-wrapped bundle. She seemed in high spirits. The Major was nowhere to be seen; he had apparently been banished to some distant part of the house. Chapdelaine, I thought, did not look well; he coughed from time to time, complained of damp sheets at the pub, and constantly piled more logs on the fire. We took several shots of them both, but Mrs. O'Shea would not allow us to see the uncompleted portrait.

"Not till it's quite done!" she said firmly. Meanwhile it stood on its easel in the corner, covered with a sheet, like some hesitant ghost.

During this time I had had numerous calls from Patrick, of course; he was wildly impatient about the slow progress of the painting.

"Do persuade Armand to go a bit faster, can't you, Ellis? He used to be able to dash off a portrait in about four sittings."

"Well, I'll pass on your message, Patrick, but people's methods change, you know."

When I rang Clayhole next day, however, I was unable to get through; the line was out of order apparently, and remained so; when I reported this to the local exchange, the girl said, "Double four six three . . . wait a minute; yes, I thought so. We had a nine-nine-nine call from them not long ago. Fire brigade. No, that's all I can tell you, I'm afraid."

With my heart in my suede boots I got out the car and drove down to Clayhole. The lane was blocked by police trucks, fire engines, and appliances; I had to leave my car at the bottom and walk up.

Clayhole was a smoking ruin; as I arrived they were just carrying the third blackened body out to the ambulance.

"What began it?" I asked the fire chief.

"That'll be for the insurance assessors to decide, miss. But it's plain it started in the lounge; spark from the fire, most likely. Wood fires are always a bit risky, in my opinion. You get that green applewood—"

A spark, of course; I thought of the jersey-wrapped pile of poems hardly a foot distant from the crackling logs.

"You didn't find any papers in that room?"

"Not a scrap, miss; that being where the fire started, everything was reduced to powder."

When Patrick got through to me that evening, he was pretty distraught.

"She planned the whole thing!" he said furiously. "I bet you, Ellis, she had it all thought out from the start. There's absolutely nothing that woman won't do to get her own way. Haven't I always said she was utterly unscrupulous? But I shan't be beaten by her, I'm just as determined as she is— *Do* pay attention, Ellis!"

"Sorry, Patrick. What were you saying?" I was very low-spirited, and his next announcement did nothing to cheer me.

"I'll dictate you the poems; it shouldn't take more than a month or so if we keep at it. We can start right away. Have you a pen? And you'll want quite a lot of paper. I've finished the volcano poem, so we may as well start with that—ready?"

"I suppose so." I shut my eyes. The cold clutch on my wrist was like a fetter. But I felt that having gone so far, I owed this last service to Patrick.

"Right—here we go." There followed a long pause. Then he said, with a good deal less certainty:

"*On each hand the flames*
Driven backward slope their pointing spires—"

"That's from *Paradise Lost*, Patrick," I told him gently.

"I know. . . ." His voice was petulant. "That isn't what I meant to say. The thing is—it's starting to get so cold here. Oh, God, Ellis—it's so *cold*. . . ."

His voice petered out and died. The grasp on my wrist became freezing, became numbing, and then, like a melted icicle, was gone.

"Patrick?" I said. "Are you there, Patrick?"

But there was no reply, and, indeed, I hardly expected one. Patrick never got through to me again. His mother had caught up with him at last.

A Taxi to Solitude

THIS is not a cheerful story. It is the record of a day last summer, the saddest, strangest day of my whole life; if I live three times as long again, there will never be another like it.

I am a Forestry Commission inspector. I had broken some bones in a felling accident and was convalescent, staying with my uncle who keeps The Vine pub at Hemingwell. I slept, and strolled about, and ate apples, and drove my uncle's taxi for him, as it was the grape harvest. Uncle William's vine—there was a real one growing all over his pub and a vineyard behind it—was of the most serious importance to him. At vintage time the whole neighbourhood was invited up to tread his grapes, with free meals at the pub. Normal village life, not to mention licensing hours, went by the board, and saturnalia—solid, happy, self-satisfied English saturnalia—took over for a few days.

In this pretty village—lilac trees, weatherboard houses, Virginia creeper turning to fire in the first autumn dews—I was content enough, cruising the massive taxi, exchanging ideas with the neighbours, when they were not too drunk to listen, feeling the hot, hop-picking sun gradually penetrate into my bones. No hint of tragedy.

The taxi was a 1910 Ramsey-Lavrock, a lovely work of art. It was built on ambitious lines with heavy wooden bodywork, a high-perched chassis approached not just by one or two steps but a whole flight, wide, cushioned leather seats like the older-fashioned station-waiting-room benches, and great brass lamps big as portholes.

Behind the passenger seats was a luggage compartment, long and wide enough to carry a sofa, its floor padded by a kind of mattress, also leather-upholstered. Over the whole vehicle was slung a fringed waterproof canopy.

I describe the taxi in such detail because it was important in what followed. I loved that absurd conveyance—if I could have persuaded Uncle William to part with it, and if there had been space to keep it, I'd have it now. It was big, reassuring, solid, handsome, and snug, just the way an old mum should be. You could have lived in that taxi.

One evening, as dusk was beginning to fall, I was down at the station yard waiting for stray custom. Lined up with the modern coupés and convertibles, the taxi looked like St. Paul's among concrete office blocks.

There were four trains a day, two up, two down, and sometimes a passenger would decide to leave the train and sniff the air of Hemingwell. On this occasion, a woman came out of the station yard and stood looking round. Then she walked towards me.

She was younger than I had thought at first; the way she moved, so elegant, so composed, had misled me. She had a cloud of dark hair and a compassionate mouth; her eyes in the shadowy light were only a blur.

"Is this a taxi?" she asked. "Can you take me to the hospital?"

Something about her voice stirred me unaccountably. I stalled, wanting her to speak again. "Hemingwell hospital, do you mean?"

There was only one in the neighbourhood. It stood at the top of the hill, on the main road, high above the village. You could see it for miles.

"Yes."

She put hardly any voice into the breathed monosyllable, but again it moved me strangely.

"Certainly," I said. I opened the heavy, brass-fitted door and she climbed up.

"I feel like the Queen of Sheba in here," she said, laughing.

A lamp hung inside the taxi, a kind of chandelier, and by its light she caught sight of my face in the doorway. Her eyes widened in astonishment.

"Why—it's *you!*"

"It's you!"

We stared at one another incredulously.

"I didn't know you drove a taxi—that wasn't what you said—" she began, and hesitated.

"I don't, normally. I'm helping my uncle; he keeps the pub here. I didn't know you were coming south; you never said . . ."

"South! Not very far south!"

"Compared with where I met you last, it is. But how extraordinary, meeting you again like this—"

"I've so often thought about you."

"Not so often as I've thought about *you.* A dozen times I've cursed myself for not getting your address. I wondered if a letter to Carsluith Post Office would find you."

"Carsluith? Why there?" She sounded puzzled.

"Wasn't that the name of the place where we met? Yes, I'm sure it was. Carsluith, on the strand."

"You're very absent-minded." She was amused again, but there was a twinge of disappointment underneath. "It wasn't Carsluith at all. I've never heard of the place. It was at the Wertheims' party last month."

"The Wertheims?"

"Yes, of course it was." Her voice was indulgent. "Don't you remember? We sat all evening in the corner behind the castor-oil plant, and you told me about your painting."

"Painting? I don't paint." More and more bewildered, I climbed onto the box, slid back the glass pane that separated us, and set the stately taxi in motion. We freewheeled through the main street of Hemingwell and turned up a side lane. "I don't paint, and I don't know any people called Wertheim."

"Oh, don't be so crazy!" She sounded quite angry now. "Of course you do! It was at their party, at their flat in Guildford Street."

"I've never been there in my life."

"Is this some stupid joke? You're pulling my leg, aren't you?" There was a note of pleading, almost of panic in her voice.

"Truly I'm not. Don't be angry," I begged. I couldn't bear that she should be angry with me. "Look, I can prove it. When was this party? What date?"

"It was on a Thursday. Let me think. Three weeks, a month ago—it must have been the thirteenth of last month. Yes, and I know it was, because I had a dentist appointment the same day. See, it's in my diary."

I halted the taxi at the top of a wooded rise where the road ran out between hop fields and there was a view of the hospital across the valley. She showed me a tiny green leather-bound diary with the words *Dentist, Wertheim,* written in for the thirteenth. Once again, as with her voice, the handwriting gave me a queer, familiar pang. I stared at the opposite hillside with dimmed eyes, seeing but not seeing the lights of the fast traffic slide beadwise along the main road.

"But you see I can't have been there! On the thirteenth of last month I was in Scotland. In fact, that might have been the very day—yes, it was actually the day—I know. Because I had to ring my uncle in the evening—"

"The very day that what?"

I had stopped speaking, unnerved by the strangeness of it.

"Why, the day that *I* was meeting *you.*"

"What *do* you mean?"

"I met you in Scotland. On the beach at Carsluith."

"But I've never been to Scotland—or not since I was a child, anyway."

"It was on the beach. At this little place, Carsluith. I was walking back across the sand, and I met you. You were wearing a grey-and-white checked dress and a blue belt. You stopped me and asked if I had seen some children and a dog. You were looking after them for a friend and you were worried because they had gone off on their own. The current there is dangerous on the ebb and they weren't allowed to bathe. I walked back with you and we found them playing on the sand; they were all right, so we sat and talked."

"It must have been someone else," she said.

"How could it have been? It was you. I'd pick you from a million."

"I've never been there."

"It was you."

"What is my name?" she said.

"Helen."

From the strangeness of the look she gave me I knew I was right. It had to be Helen. I couldn't have made a mistake. Helen was the only name for her.

"And mine?"

"—I don't know. You didn't tell me. You said no one ever used it. But that was at this party—at the Wertheims'." Her voice rose. "You *must* have been there! You must be pulling my leg."

"There's an easy way to find out," I suggested. "Ring up the Wertheims and ask if I was there. There's a call box by the hospital."

I told her my name—the name my friends never use. We were silent for the rest of the drive, half angry with each other, half afraid. I pulled up by the call box, thrust a hand into my pocket, and offered her a palm full of change. She shook her head, jumped down decisively, and crossed to the booth. While she stood in it waiting for her number, I watched her, illuminated as she was by the overhead light, with the queerest feeling I'd ever had. She seemed so familiar, so unaccountably dear—and yet all the evidence showed that we'd never met before.

She came out looking white and shaken.

"Well? What did they say?"

"Julius Wertheim says I spent the whole evening talking to his sister and his old aunt. He says he has never heard of you." Her eyes met mine with a kind of piteous accusation.

"Well, at least I wasn't gatecrashing," I said, trying to be jaunty.

A bell began to ring inside the hospital.

"Oh, goodness! That must be the end of visiting hours, and I haven't even been in. What shall I do?"

"Better skip it this time," I suggested. "Who were you visiting?"

"A girl I've never met. I belong to a Society of Friends, and we arrange to visit lonely people in hospital with no relatives of their own."

"Well, if you've never met her, she won't miss one evening."

"No, I suppose not," she said doubtfully. "I must make sure of going tomorrow. Can I stay down here somewhere?"

"Why, yes. My uncle will put you up at The Vine. But now get back in and let me go on driving you round. We've got nothing sorted yet."

"I don't see how we ever can," she said in a despairing voice. I helped her up and she sat beside me on the front seat. "I remember you and you remember me, but we seem to be remembering two different people, not each other at all."

Quite suddenly she began to cry, staring down at her clenched hands in her lap. Tears rolled one after another down her cheeks and she made no effort to stop them.

I hesitated, longing to put an arm round her, uncertain, so odd was the link between us, how this would be taken.

"It sounds stupid," she brought out presently between sobs, "but I'm going to miss you so! At that party—we seemed—we seemed—to have established something so close between us. And now to find that the whole thing was a dream—didn't exist—"

"But *I* exist," I said. "And you exist."

She drew a deep, quivering sigh, and after a moment pulled out a hankerchief and wiped her eyes. The old taxi rumbled its way down the hospital drive. Gentle autumn rain whispered on the broad yellowing leaves of the chestnuts, which turned and flashed in the light of our carriage lamps. Showers of drops pattered on the canopy over our heads.

"You said you were a painter. You talked about visual harmonics. What *do* you do if you don't paint?"

"I have a job. Unexciting. Perhaps I'll start painting some day, who knows?"

"What did *I* talk about? On that beach of yours?"

"Shells," I said. "And the sea. You told me all the different names of the shells—whelks, limpets, cowries—I'd never heard them before."

A dreadful pang of loss shook me as I remembered her hands holding the shells on the grey-and-white lap of her dress, and her peaceful, happy voice: "The children love these because of their pink linings. The science of shells is called conchology, did you know? . . ."

I looked at the girl by my side. She was frowning, the puzzled crease between her brows was outlined by the yellow light from the lamps.

"I don't know anything about shells," she said wearily. "It can't really have been either of us, can it? And yet it seems so unfair. As if it had been *meant* for us. If only it had been."

"Why 'if only'?"

"Because then," she said simply, "we should neither of us ever have to be lonely again."

"Are we lonely?"

"You know we are."

"But, Helen—"

She looked at me doubtfully.

"Well?"

"This is us now."

"It is? Can we be sure? Can we be sure that in a month's time we shan't meet again and be strangers somewhere else?"

"Then we should waste no time now," I said.

Her shadowed eyes in the uncertain light raised so questioningly, the sight of her face so close to mine ached in me like a hunger. I took her in my arms. She resisted a moment, then relaxed against me with a small, forlorn sigh. Her mouth turned to mine.

The old cab rested tranquilly in the shelter of a hazel copse.

"I wanted to do this in Scotland," I told her after a while. "But I didn't dare."

"I did too. At the party. I hoped you'd offer to take me home. But you just got up and went quickly out as if you'd suddenly remembered something. You didn't even say good-bye. You won't do that again, will you?" She tightened her clasp on my hand. "What did I do? In Scotland?"

"One of the children, the smallest one, cut his foot, and you said you must take him home. You waved good-bye and called that we'd probably meet the next day. I looked and looked for you every day after that, asked people where you lived, but nobody knew."

Her lips travelled over my face like dividers over a familiar map.

"Shall I tell you something? You have a scar on your neck, below your ear. It's too dark to see it now, but I noticed it at the party."

"Yes," I said. "I got it when I was a child."

Her straying fingers found the scar.

"It really is you?"

"Who else could it be?"

After that we were silent for a long time.

Presently I said, "We should be going back and booking you a room at my uncle's pub. You must be hungry and tired."

"I don't want to," she said obstinately. "I'd much rather stay here. I don't want to meet other people, ordinary people."

"We can hardly stay in this wood for ever."

"I wish we could. I've never lived in a dream before. I wish there weren't such things as houses and streets and front doors and—and tables and chairs and knives and forks."

"We can do without the knives and forks a while longer," I said, remembering. "I've a loaf and some cheese and a bottle of wine in the back. I was planning to knock off after a couple of fares and eat my supper down in the hop fields."

The rain had stopped momentarily. I took out one of the wide leather cushions from the passenger seat, and we ate under a hazel bush, in the golden glimmer of the lamps, nibbling cheese and breaking the bread in our fingers, drinking wine from the silver flower cup, which was one of the lavish appointments of that wonderful taxi.

"It's like being at home, isn't it?" said Helen, looking up at the scalloped edge of canopy against the ragged leaf shadows. She leaned back against a mossy stump and I put my head in her lap.

"Perhaps this is our home. We could stay here. We could sleep in the cab."

After a while the pattering on the leaves began again, and so we moved into the luggage compartment and there, covered with a rug, went to sleep in each other's arms, our dreams accompanied by the rain's drip and whisper on the oiled silk over our heads.

"I wonder who you really are?" murmured Helen, just before her eyes closed. "The you of Scotland or the you of London?"

"Both. Perhaps there are four people in the cab, not two."

It didn't seem like four. In the leafy dark, close together, we seemed not even like two people, but like one.

Next morning was golden and September hot. We finished the loaf for breakfast with handfuls of blackberries.

"I hate having to go back to the real world."

"Even for coffee and a shave?"

"Even for champagne and a Turkish bath."

Hemingwell was hardly the real world. When at length we did cruise the taxi down the leaf-swept cobbles to The Vine, we found wine treading in full swing. We received absent-minded smiles and courteous vague greetings from my preoccupied uncle and his neighbours as they hurried about with jugs and basins, pestles and mortars.

The housekeeper showed Helen a room and gave us some lunch. We wandered in the vineyard and the hop fields and threw raisins to my uncle's flashing pheasants in their pens.

Dusk overtook us before we expected it, and with an armful of roses for the girl in the hospital we went out to the taxi in The Vine courtyard. It welcomed us like an old nurse in an Elizabethan play, spacious and gracious and knowing.

During the day we had not talked much. We held hands—Helen's were small and cool—and I found an old signet ring that she could wear on her first finger. We were silent on the drive to the hospital.

Near the turn into the main road I said, "I'll wait for you outside. Do you think we might go up to the hazel wood again afterwards?"

And Helen answered, rather oddly, I thought, "Twice? Don't you think twice in a lifetime might be too much to expect?"

At that moment the Mercedes hit us, hurtling round the bend, out of control, at over seventy miles an hour.

I was thrown clear. Helen was not.

Help, of course, came quickly. We were only a few yards from the hospital gates, and the crash could have been heard from there to Brighton. They were on the spot with stretchers almost before the wheels of the upside-down Mercedes stopped turning. The taxi was matchwood.

As soon as I came to after they had set my broken legs, I asked about Helen.

A nurse called a Sister, who called a doctor.

"Are you a friend?" he asked. He was a gray-haired man, kind and tired and troubled.

"I'm going to marry her."

"Oh. Oh, I see." His distress deepened. "I—I have to tell you that she is not expected to recover consciousness. And, in a way, it's merciful. There's nothing we can do for her except deaden the pain."

I looked at him numbly for a while, and then said, "Can I be with her?"

They carried me in. She was lying in a screened side ward. Someone had rescued the roses, not much battered, and put them in a white jug on the windowsill. Helen lay very quietly, her head turned on one side as if she were sleeping.

I sat there in a sling chair and listened to the hospital noises ebb and flow. I wondered about the girl Helen had been going to visit—did she know what had happened? I wondered about the driver of the Mercedes, and how my uncle was getting on with his vintage.

At half-past three she moved a hand slowly from under the masking sheet, and whispered, as if to herself, "Children . . . love these ones with pink linings. Did you know . . . the science of shells . . . was called conchology?"

Five minutes later she died without, as they had prophesied, having recovered consciousness. I sat beside her for the rest of the night, though they wanted to move me.

When they finally allow me out of hospital, I am going to learn painting. There's a picture I have, somehow, to get onto canvas while it is still fresh in my memory: *Portrait of a Girl with Shells.*